Pmegranate

A Novel

Weam Namou

HERMiZ
PUBLiSHING

ISBN: 978-1-945371-00-4

Library of Congress Cataloging-in-Publication Data
2020925301

Namou, Weam
Pomegranate
(fiction)
First Edition
Published in the United States of America by:
Hermiz Publishing, Inc.
Sterling Heights, MI
10 9 8 7 6 5 4 3 2 1

Acknowledgements

My thanks to Thomas Mitz, who called me one day out of the blue and suggested I write a story about Iraqi refugees, reminding me of a script I had tucked away in my files and inspiring me to transform it into a modern-day tale; Elisabeth Kahn, for lending an ear over tea and coffee as we discussed the cultural topics in *Pomegranate*; Dr. Stanley Williams, for his enduring mentorship, friendship, and his invaluable story-telling guidance.

Foreword

The book you hold in your hands, or on your electronic tablet, is something that has brewed in Weam's Enheduanna spirit for years. *Pomegranate*, although presented as a work of fiction, is in many ways not fiction at all. In human terms, it is biographical and about the many people she knows socially, professionally and those she has interviewed and written about across multiple continents in her decades long career. *Pomegranate* is also autobiographical for she has lived through many of the scenes portrayed.

Whereas "Historical Fiction" weaves and juxtaposes real events and places with the fictional characters, *Pomegranate* is "Real-Life Fiction." Sterling Heights and Little Baghdad really exist. The houses Weam describes with the garage doors that face the street with an "attitude" really exist. When the garage doors lift-up they really do reveal kitchen appliances in the back and living room furniture that sits facing the street. That there are homes occupied by Chaldean (Iraqi Christians) with Virgin Mary statues and Trump-Pence signs across the street from Iraqi Muslims who are new to the United States and fear the Trump deportation squads...is, unfortunately, more real than it should be.

Yet, throughout Sterling Heights (and I've been there many times), Muslims, Jews, and Christians get along famously. There are no cultural riots in Sterling Heights although the city council meetings could become a TV reality series. Sterling Heights is a comfortable and safe, suburban community just north of Detroit. It has all the amenities, conveniences, services, entertainment, and shopping districts middle-America would ever imagine. There are Mosques, Synagogues and Churches throughout the area, and the congregants all live on the same streets, shop in the same places, and play in the same parks.

How is that possible? Very simply because there are many people —Muslims, Jews, and Christians—like Weam Namou who understand the wealth of riches that diverse cultures bring to a community, and who work hard to accentuate those virtues. That is what makes the United State of America a valued place to live, work, worship, and raise a family.

And perhaps that's the point of *Pomegranate's* story. Nisreen describes it at the end when she slices open a pomegranate and reveals the membranes and sweet, juicy seeds. She says, "We are all God's children here on Earth…all of whom are precious."

The story of *Pomegranate* has always intrigued me. On one hand, it's a story of assimilation, where the alien traits of a distant culture learn to meld into an existing one. But it is also a story of integration where the diversity of many different cultures blend, merge, coalesce, commingle… and fuse into a new one.

I'm thrilled to see the story get told and told well by a prolific creator with a deep sense of humor and human insight.

Stanley D. Williams, PhD
author of *The Moral Premise: Harnessing Virtue & Vice for Box Office Success*

Books by

Weam Namou

The Feminine Art

The Mismatched Braid

The Flavor of Cultures

I Am a Mute Iraqi with a Voice

The Great American Family: A Story of Political Disenchantment

Iraqi Americans: The War Generation

Iraqi Americans: Witnessing a Genocide

Iraqi Americans: The Lives of the Artists

Healing Wisdom for a Wounded World: My Life-Changing Journey
Through a Shamanic School (Book 1)

Healing Wisdom for a Wounded World: My Life-Changing Journey
Through a Shamanic School (Book 2)

Healing Wisdom for a Wounded World: My Life-Changing Journey
Through a Shamanic School (Book 3)

Healing Wisdom for a Wounded World: My Life-Changing Journey
Through a Shamanic School (Book 4)

Mesopotamian Goddesses: Unveiling Your Feminine Power

Chapter 1

Niran Al Mousawi stood in front of the mirror one gray morning, in the middle of her simple and sparingly furnished bedroom. The light streaming in from a solitary window was unflattering, which she noticed while modeling her fashionable, black, chiffon hijab. At twenty years old, she was filled with determination and did not underestimate the symmetry of her curves, the fairness of her youthful skin and its subsequent glow, and the brilliance of her large, hazel eyes, which, with no makeup, easily caught the attention of men and women. There was no need for modesty.

A November 2016 calendar hung on the wall with the first and second days marked off with big red Xs. Next to the calendar were pictures of the Virgin Mary, Jesus, and Imam Hussein, all wearing headscarves. All of them somber and present, as if waiting for something to change. It never did.

On the bookshelf attached to her pine, merlot-colored bed were minimal but important selections on Ancient Mesopotamia, Sumerian poetry, and a biography of the famed priestess Enheduanna, the first recorded writer in history. She would always glance at the titles when she woke up as if involuntarily saying hello to them when the day began.

Sitting on her bed, Niran closed and set aside a thick book on Babylonian history, her bookmark placed in the first quarter. She put on her headphones, pressed the screen on her iPhone to start an American song, and lay down on her bed, on her stomach so she could write. She was moved by the remarkable voice of Gethen Christine, a local artist who poured her heart out through her lyrics. Gethen spoke of the holiest of lights, in the darkest hours of hope, in the brightest times of dreams, in the dawn's waking light, in the sacred mystery.

As the music faltered, slow and drastic, Niran composed some poetry in her journal, stopping here and there to ruminate along the way.

> *I am a rebel child.*
> *My body, my voice!*
> *Don't tell me what to cover.*
> *Or what to leave exposed.*
> *Don't tell me what I need.*
> *Or how to wear my clothes.*

She held up her iPhone, pretending to record a video of a performance that was filled with utopian kingdoms and progressive, innovative lifestyle alternatives, intellectual realms, and mystical musings. She imagined it all in her mind, the thoughts creating images coming out from the corners of her mind, creating art as they manifested.

She flew higher and higher in her head, leaving behind the people she lived with—her mother and father and her younger brother and sister; leaving behind her American city, nicknamed "Little Baghdad", due to its large Iraqi American population. At every corner, there was a family-owned produce market that had a tandoor that made a variety of Iraqi bread each morning, such as *samoon* and *khoubuz*.

It was like a homeland on alien ground, an Iraq within the States. There were ample Iraqi restaurants like Baghdad, Ishtar, the Jasmin Mediterranean Grill, and Al Masgouf, to name a few. There were the bakeries—Baghdad Tower Sweets and Farhat Sweets and other businesses with English and Arabic signets lined up on the streets, selling delicious sweets and savories all year round.

Sterling Heights sat on Earth like a pebble on the moon, with branches of the Clinton River flowing through it. Its ranch-style, suburban houses appeared to be built on the same plan, like dominos stacked together in mediocrity, with their garage doors confronting the street with the attitude of old wisdom.

Niran left it all behind, or at least she tried to, since most often, such as at the present moment, she did not go very far, and immersed herself into formulating words, wanting more—more than this cynical, critical, simpler existence.

My parents wanted a boy
(As all of them do)
Instead, they got a girl:
A girl who has the heart and brain of a
thousand men, the extraordinary
design of a warrior,
the fearlessness of a jungle cat.
Push me down and tell me I can't do it,
and I will prove you wrong once again!
My parents wanted a boy
(As they all do)
Instead, they got a warrioress.

She imagined the thousands, maybe even millions, of Facebook likes that she would one day receive. She continued to rehearse her thoughts and feelings through verbal gestures, gesticulating, creating, just with her mind, the way the Mesopotamian poet Enheduanna claimed her fame. Enheduanna was the first known author in the world because she decided to sign her name on her work, something that had never been done before. This made her hymns significant for centuries.

Niran melted into those thoughts; she would be a poet, a performer, an entertainer, and she would move millions. Her constant *This will be me one day!* view of herself grew as she continued to write.

I don't identify myself with the people of this house.
In the morning, I claim the title of a Judaea-Christian.
By evening, that of a Shia-Sufi-Muslim.
By night, I am free to fall asleep
with the handsome shining sky,
without the labels the world wants to place upon me,
while covered in God's countless blessings.

Suddenly, the door burst open, startling her. She turned to see the sight of Ali, her tall and handsome younger brother, who had evidently been eavesdropping. It was an immature habit which made him, in Niran's opinion, resemble a prepubescent boy rather than a 19-year-old man. But then again, boys never grew up. They never had to.

"*Walla*, your philosophy is very good," he said, leaning against the door frame, his iPhone attached to his hand like a tattoo. He smiled at her in an unsightly manner, unnerving her. "Can I buy it on Amazon?"

4

Ali followed his comment up with hysterical laughter, which made Niran think of a hyena in the wilderness. She grabbed a pillow, threw it at him, and demanded that he get out. He laughed even harder as he closed the door, clearly unfazed.

Typical of him. She stared at the door, disgusted at how fast she turned from a poetic priestess into an angry adolescent. If only she could escape from this world's time-worn traditions and transform her humdrum routine, then she could live out her cherished dreams and ideals. If only she could be free.

Before she could return to her poetry, she heard her mother calling her name. She groaned out loud, her phone falling to the bed. The sound of "Niran! Niran!" felt cumbersome because labor was often associated with it. *Niran, do this, do that. Niran, I need this, go here, go there. Niran! Niran! Niran!* At times, her name no longer felt like it belonged to her. It was an annoying sound, repetitive and brash, like fingernails on a chalkboard.

Niran placed her journal and pen on the bookshelf near her bed. She got up and undid her fashionable hijab to wear the house one, which was pink with brown hues, lightweight and more convenient to slip on and off. She often slept with it on and typically removed her hijabs on two major occasions: to take a shower or to brush her hair.

She began to leave the room, but stopped for a moment to glance out of her front window. She could just see the outline of a house across the street that was almost identical to hers. She leaned forward to see the entrance.

Striding out of the front doorway was Mary, an elegant, long-haired, young Iraqi-American woman who was only a year older than Niran. Ready for work in fashionable clothes, she stepped up to a large, classic, blue-robed Virgin Mary statue installed next to a "TRUMP: Make America Great Again" sign. She kissed the Virgin's statue, made the sign of the cross, and headed to her car parked in the driveway. It also boldly displayed a "TRUMP/PENCE" sticker.

Niran glanced at her laptop over the bed and changed her mind. She would not oblige her mother just yet. There were better things to be done. She sat on the bed and stared at her Facebook page, bright and open for display. She typed words as she uttered them aloud in a poetic voice, getting back into the zone.

There are always two Marys on this earth:
One; the Mother, the Virgin, praised, revered, compared to doves
and lilies and perfection.
The other; the Lover, the Wanted, burdened with the weight of
men's sins, in the depth of their own guilt and desire.

She looked out the window once again, and this time she saw Mary's older brother, Matthew, roll a trash receptacle to the curb. Her heart sped up at the sight of him walking across the lawn, swept away by this handsome and shy 23-year-old the moment he came into her peripheral vision. She bit her lip as he threw away the garbage and wiped his brow with the back of his arm, the sweat rolling down his neck. He was such a distraction.

She shook the image of him off and looked back at her laptop. Her hand hesitated before decisively clicking share, and she saw her post join the rest of the edited lives that distorted peoples' perception of reality. She loved it—all of it in its mess and chaos. Competing for attention, the incoming array of reactions, the likes, and dislikes, how the press of a button could make people happy, unhappy, informed, misinformed, satisfied, angry, bewildered. Facebook gave her power. Her only power.

In another area of the small house, in the attached garage, the garage door lifted, allowing sunlight into a full kitchen. The clean appliances gleamed in the rear, and the living room furniture, placed in the front, was facing the street. There was no room left for what the garage was intended for—a parked car.

Niran's mother, Hassina, put a pomegranate on a cutting board and began to slice it with a meat cleaver. A large, 45-year-old woman, she always dressed in a hijab, a floral muumuu, sandals, and gold bracelets her husband had bought her in Iraq, as part of her dowry, decades ago. She was rough-looking and disgruntled, worn out from the wars of men, displacement, and migration, garnished with the status of a refugee.

Like a number of her Iraqi neighbors, she used her garage as an impromptu kitchen to mix and heat ingredients, especially for elaborate Iraqi dishes that require long hours of preparation and an overworked oven. Having a parked car in there was the last thing she would have bothered with. Using kitchen appliances in the garage also prevented certain odors from sticking to the inside of the house walls, the way perfume sticks to fabric. In particular: fish, falafel, fried potato patties, fried eggplants, fried zucchini, or anything that required frying.

In some homes, the garage was used as a hangout place, with a few families choosing to replace the current garage door with a sliding door. But doing so only ended with them gaining the attention of officials wanting to change ordinances.

Ali came behind his mother and kissed her cheek. He grabbed a slice of the pomegranate and bit into it. Seeds spilled everywhere, except on his iPhone, which he protected instinctively. Hassina shooed him away and slapped the back of his neck.

"You think this is funny, huh?" she scolded, pinching her fingers together. "Okay, Ali, okay!"

"Mom, why are you freaking out?" Ali asked nonchalantly.

"Did you say the F-word?" she asked, horrified at the type of people her children were turning into.

Ali shook his head. "What? Mom, no, I said-"

Before he could finish, his mother took off her sandal and threw it at him. He ducked and ran into the house, thinking of the offensive symbolism the sole of a sandal or shoe had in Arab culture. He also thought of what he did to deserve it.

In the Muslim faith, shoes need to be removed before prayer and before entering a mosque. Crossing your ankle over a knee and displaying the shoe's sole while talking to someone is insulting. The shoe is, well, dirty. It is on the ground and associated with the foot, the lowest part of the body. So, hitting someone with a shoe shows the victim is regarded as even lower than dirt. It's the ultimate insult, sort of. For Muslim mothers, it is a weapon. That was why Ali had chosen to become an atheist and sever ties from Arab traditions. Something his mother did not need to know.

When the noise her son had caused departed, Hassina

brought out eggs and date syrup from the garage's refrigerator to make breakfast. She cooked absorbingly, falling into the activity of moving meticulously and cleanly. Like most Iraqi women, she was fond of food and Mesopotamian culinary arts, which had a history dating back to 10,000 years. It stemmed from cuneiform tablets found in ancient ruins in Iraq, showing recipes in the temples during religious festivals, making them the first cookbooks in the world. Of course, Hassina didn't know all that. She simply carried the truth of it in her genes, dutifully claiming her role in the kitchen, or in some cases the garage, instead of in the world.

"Tell your sister, I need her," she said, as Ali walked away from the garage kitchen and entered the house, laughing at the incident.

Things like this were bound to happen every other morning, he thought, and for the most part, he wasn't bothered by them. But soon enough, reality set in, and he became annoyed. The list of dos and don'ts in this family prevented him from enjoying the wildness of the nights associated with the American dream—the stuff he saw in the movies and TV shows. There was so much that was not allowed and downright forbidden.

He asked himself a number of questions. Did the American dream really exist, or was it simply a modern fairy tale, silly and cute, but far from reality? Was it not worthy of his attention to uphold the American dream, or was he to yield to his parents' impression of the definition of democracy? Was he not an American boy? Ali pondered over these thoughts, wondering if they were too deep to deal with, and found ways to distract himself. He barged into Niran's room, pomegranate seeds stuck onto his stubbly chin.

"Mom's calling you," he said plainly.

Niran didn't respond and continued to do what she was doing before he intruded. She recorded spoken-word poetry by clicking the Facebook Live button, except she wasn't actually recording right now.

Woman, she must restrain, preserve herself for the ultimate man,
the one who will become her Groom, or more precisely, Her Master.
But is she a jar of pickles or jam, to be preserved, not human with
a collection of feelings?
Is she not brilliant, engaging, and articulate, made to enjoy life,
blossom, and create?

"Who are you talking to?" Ali asked.

Niran lowered her phone and glared at him.

"I'm practicing my Facebook Live."

Ali opened up Facebook on his phone to check out his sister's activity.

"You crazy?" he asked, his eyes wandering over the stream. "Dude. Mom and Dad know about this?"

"I'm just practicing, not actually doing it yet," she said, her voice laced with sarcasm. "Allah knows you'd be the first human to know."

"They already hate hearing about the crap you post. Now you want people to see you saying it?"

"I'm going to be a Facebook warrior… for women… and it's not crap," Niran insisted, clearly agitated.

"More like a keyboard warrior. It's all bullshit," Ali replied, putting his phone away. He ran his hand over his chin, pushing away the seeds stuck on it. His fingers came away sticky, making him squirm.

She looked up. "Lord, deliver him from this stupidity."

"Get your ass off Facebook and go see what Mom wants."

Ali left the room and shut the door, thinking about how absurd his sister was. On the one hand, she wanted to save the world. On the other hand, she was nasty and aggressive while she tried to do it. It was why he chose to be an atheist.

As a child, he knew God was not dumb. Even God knew people babbled memorized words, they thought little about, in the name of religion. People tried to outsmart God into doing them favors through sweet talk, cajoling the empty air next to the prayer mats and inside mosques. In his teenage years, Ali saw God as the One who knew the needs of everyone and trusted them to leave everything in His hands, even during wars and chaos. But it wasn't that simple.

Later, when his mind became more curious, and he started to question more, the violence in his birth country escalated and surprised him. He began to question how the universe was created and how and why did life begin. He did not receive an answer and searched for evidence to support the idea of an all-knowing God. Instead, he found continuous disappointment in the form of horrific wars and genocides, brutal dictators and diseases, heart-wrenching genetic mutations, freak accidents, and thousands of fundamental, dumbass religions on this planet.

He again asked himself a series of questions. If he, a mere mortal, could not handle the sight of the world's present condition, how could God, the omniscient, all-loving, all-powerful, accept it? What kind of a God would let this happen? Why did He require constant prayer, praise, and rituals from people, and why did He respond to some prayers and not others? Were the starving children and helpless women not praying hard enough?

Again, there were no answers to his questions, and every cleric was too tone-deaf to help him. So, Ali decided that God was a lie that humans made up and circulated for thousands of years, that organized religion was propaganda and falsehood, that humans were flawed and disruptive. And it would always be this way.

With her brother gone, Niran stopped glowering at the door and turned back to her laptop. Picking up where she had left off when she was interrupted, she typed intensely, trying to get out as much as possible before her mother called for her again.

My family's ways want to take away my play.
They wish to bundle up my curiosity
and hand it as supper to the bees
rather than let it be set free.
They want to smother and take and lessen the essence of what will
make me grow and blossom into my soul's purpose.
It's like cutting down majestic, eon old oak trees
and depriving the forest of its canopy.

Niran reviewed what she wrote, smiled, and clicked share. Now it was time to finally leave the room, which did not feel right to her. It felt awful to abandon the pleasures of writing poetry, where rules could be broken, and she could play with words whichever way she wanted, where she could be raw and vulnerable at the same time, to go and be a perfect, obedient daughter. This sophisticated yet straightforward literature for her was the House of God, and her mother's careful eyes were the Gates of Hell.

Chapter 2

Niran lifted the heavy weight of her resistance, like one lifts a sack of rice, and forgot who she was. She left her little temple to head for the cooking galley where Fatima, her nine-year-old sister, sat at the kitchen table. Fatima was eating breakfast and playing with a lipstick tube, her small eyes idle and curious at the same time. She ate slowly, awfully slowly, and despite her young age, Niran found her habits to be irksome. She was a cute child with a quick gaze and a sharp mouth. Fatima was also the only female in the house who didn't wear a hijab. She was too young to entertain that custom and proud not to have to wear it yet.

Hassina entered the kitchen from the garage with a tray of sliced pomegranates. Niran made her arrival from her bedroom and caught a glimpse of the shiny, red seeds, glistening like jewels. Then she eyed a tray of prepared vegetables on the island, in their full color, reminding her of the dreadful work ahead. A flood of thoughts galloped into her head. Men and women were capable of performing the same household tasks, though they may operate somewhat differently. Why then did men and women not perform the same household tasks, and instead, this was a responsibility reserved for women? Did men not have the skills to peel and cut vegetables?

Niran preferred not to engage in this domestic work,

to remove the customs, traditions, norms, and expectations that had been designated to her gender. She saw domestic work as a means of undervaluing her abilities and a way for the opposite sex to demean her skills and intelligence.

"Braid your sister's hair," Hassina said to Niran. "She'll be late for school, and we have lots of work ahead of us. I want to start on the *dolma*, make *turshi*, and I thought since it's a nice day today, we can make *masgouf*, then…"

"Mom, it's not even 7:30 in the morning, and all you're thinking about is food. Stuffed vegetables, pickles, and fish, to top it off?" Niran asked, rolling her eyes.

Hassina glared at Fatima, who was still playing with the lipstick, and said to Niran, "Mamma, *habbibti*, how many times have I told you that without food, we'd starve." Her eyes, still on the lipstick, narrowed, and she asked Fatima sternly, "Where did you get that?"

"It's mine," Niran responded, giving her mother a disapproving glance. "I bought it from Amazon. For fun," she added, shrugging her shoulders.

"Allah ordered us not to change our appearance," Hassina asserted, as she opened the refrigerator. It was so packed that two heads of lettuce tumbled out, chased by a pomegranate. Niran hustled to pick them up and return the lost food.

"And more importantly," Hassina went on, "if you didn't know how to cook, who would want to marry you?"

Here we go again.

"How did the subject of food turn into marriage?" Niran asked, annoyed already.

"What girl, in her right mind, doesn't dream of marriage?"

Niran struggled to brush her sister's long and coarse, dark hair with a small comb. "Me! I've told you, again and again, I don't want to get married. Some of us have bigger dreams than men and their servitude."

"Oh, really? Then what are you going to do with your life?"

"I'm going to be a journalist," Niran said, dreamily. "No, a poetic warrior for women, a modern-day Enheduanna." She continued in a poetic rhythm:

Be it known that I will roar
Be it known with flashing eyes
You will hear me everywhere

"Maybe I can even be a rapper," she said uncertainly, as she finished her poem.

"What's a robber?" Hassina asked, her voice laced with worry. "Please tell me you will not steal for a living, my child."

"No, Mamma. Rapper. Like a singer."

Hassina slapped her right cheek in anguish. "La hawla wala quwwata illah billah!" she said, a phrase that meant there was no power and no strength except in Allah, and a person's admission that he or she was unable to do anything without the help and support of God. It was also a means for warding off the devil.

She grabbed the *hamsa*, her favorite, palm-shaped amulet, and spun it over Niran's head to scare off evil spirits. "When I tell you who called for you, you won't want no robber nonsense."

Oh, my God, not this again, Niran thought, as she waited for the inevitable, where her mother offered her a suitor on a silver platter—probably with a garnish of parsley, olives, and humus. Within Islamic law, a pure, decent marriage was structured on the basic unit of human society and laid the family's foundation. Allah mandated marriage for the believers for three simple reasons: to allow a man and a woman to live together and experience love and happiness; to produce children and provide a stable and virtuous environment for their upbringing; additionally, to provide a legal union that protects society from moral and social deprivation.

"Tell me then, who did call?" Niran asked, entertaining her mother's ideas, even if they were ridiculous.

"Someone who is tall, white, and works hard."

Niran glanced across the room. "Like our refrigerator?"

Ali snuck into the room for more pomegranate slices. Hassina shooed him away, then hollowed out a zucchini with a corer, expertly twisting and pulling the corer to scrape out the flesh, making sure not to poke the bottom of the fruit.

"Stop your foolishness," she said to Niran. "Did you read the letter that we received yesterday?"

"Can I have a pomegranate?" Fatima asked, her mouth already watering as she eyed the red fruit that looked like it was pregnant with hundreds of rubies to her.

"What letter?" Niran asked her mother, her brow furrowing.

"You didn't read it? The letter from Obama," Hassina said, and turned to Fatima. "No, you can't. It'll stain your clothes. Wait after school."

"Then why did you slice it now?" Fatima asked.

"Not now, Fatima," Hassina hushed exasperatedly, and then turned to Niran again. "Well?"

"It's something about our food stamps," Niran said,

understanding what her mother meant as she picked the letter from the rest of the mail pile on the counter and glanced over its contents.

"Our food stamps!" Hassina gasped, slapping her cheek again. She came over to look at the letter in her daughter's hands. "What about them?"

Niran clammed up, trying her best to avoid saying something rash and making the entire matter more dramatic than it needed to be. In her house, this could happen at the drop of a pin. The truth differed from reality, but speaking the truth would make her mother act out in unpleasant ways. Embarrassed that her family received food stamps, she wanted to elevate their social status and get off the subsistence, so she often pretended that she couldn't read their letters.

"You didn't read it, did you?" Hassina asked, threatening her with the corer.

Niran looked down, nervous, wondering how on earth her mother saw through the bullshit. *Just how? Did she wear a hidden gadget on her forehead which detected lies, turning their eyes yellow and their tongue blue?*

"I tried to read it," Niran lied, her voice fading, evading her mother's eyes, "but it seemed too confusing."

Hassina eyed her suspiciously. "Mamma, listen, you know I'm better than the FBI, even the ZIA, right? Nothing goes past me. Now, how could this letter be confusing? You know to read English, no? You studied in Iraq, yes? You watch YouTube all day, no? How could you not understand what this says?"

"Mom, I barely started college before the damn ISIS wrecked our lives."

"Oh, blame ISIS!" Hassina looked to the sky with open

arms. "Thanks to Allah, I was smart enough not to waste time on education." She returned her ferocious gaze on Niran. "Are words too big for you? Why didn't you look them up on the computer? You're on Vazeboog all day doing tick, tick, tick…" Hassina imitated someone typing, her hips following her body movement, left, right, left, right, as zucchini flesh dripped from the corer. She looked like a comical cartoon character.

Part of Niran wanted to laugh, the other part wanted to cry. She did neither and went back to Fatima to silently finish braiding her sister's hair. At that moment, her father, Sermad, ambled into the kitchen. Niran adored her father, who was a 48-year-old, easy-going, teddy bear of a man. He dressed semi-well for work and visitors, but around the house he was fond of wearing old T-shirts and low-riding pants that didn't cover his round belly.

Sermad was not quite as lazy and lax as he appeared, but that was how he looked to most people even though he was the only person in the house with a job. He worked full-time as a cashier at a grocery store, and his pay was barely enough to cover the house rent and utility bills. He dreamt of one day having a second car so that his son could get a job too, and help support the family, although his wife, who had done some serious calculations, had warned that their financial situation would likely worsen if a second household member worked. Basically, that their food stamps would be cut off.

Sermad squeezed Niran's shoulder. She was glad for the distraction.

"Good morning, Babba," he said, smiling widely.

"Hi, Babba. You want a cup of tea?"

"Yes, Babba."

"Mamma and Babba, why do you call us kids Mamma and Babba if we're not your Mamma and Babba?" Fatima asked, with wide eyes and a curious expression.

Sermad kissed Fatima's head and sat at the table. He grabbed the Kroger sales circular and skimmed through it. "What kind of question is that?" he asked, as he put on his reading glasses.

"It's like confusing," said Fatima.

Hassina pointed the corer at Fatima. "Mamma, habbibti, I love you. You're my life, my eyes, my soul, but you better be good in school so you can become a dactoor. Any other profession, like robber, and…" Hassina eyed Niran as she moved her hand across her throat. "I mean, anything else will just not do."

Unfortunately for the child, there was no answer that her father could give because he and his wife were not the type to look into the history and culture of such matters. In their mind, life was what it was. Things were the way they were, and no questioning was allowed. Unless you were the captain and could steer it, there was no sense in rocking the boat and sinking it. If you insisted on rocking the boat, you should at least have hired or rented a captain—a friendly and experienced one—or studied to become a captain.

So, for the Al Mousawee parents, rather than explain that "Mamma" and "Babba" were emotional phrases expressing love and affection, there just wasn't an explanation. Instead of telling the child that the phrase was shortened from "yes, who is the beloved of Mamma or Babba," they simply ignored the question.

"You still didn't answer my question," the child persisted, not comprehending the extent of her parents' obliviousness.

"Some things don't have an answer," her father replied.

"And other things are more important to answer," said Hassina. "Like the letter!"

"What letter?" Sermad asked, scratching his head as he looked at his wife.

"A letter from Obama," Hassina said, hollowing out the zucchini, this time with an anger and crude impatience that caused a hole at the bottom. She cussed beneath her breath. "Niran, get me the letter. I'll take it to the neighbors across the street."

"Mom, no! Don't take it to them," Niran said. She then placed a cup of tea on the table in front of Sermad, who promptly leaned back and held the cup up with one hand and the Kroger circular with the other hand. He looked peaceful for a second.

"Why?" Hassina asked. "What's wrong with *them?*"

"I can't stand that Mary! She acts like we're beneath her."

"We kind of are," Hassina said. "She's been in America decades longer, and you don't know as good English as she does."

"She posts tons of biblical verses on Facebook when I know she's far from being a Mother Teresa."

"Better than the junk you post, telling people they're doomasses and product of camouflage and incest if they disagree with you. Every day I get a call from Auntie Akila complaining about your Vazeboog garbage."

"That's because most of our relatives are ghetto."

Hassina looked up with open arms. "Allah, what sins have I committed to deserve this ungrateful daughter who can't even read a letter from Obama?"

21

"Groger has a special on chuck roast," Sermad said, reading the ad. "Buy one, get one free."

"Babba, how many times have I told you, it's Kroger, not Groger?"

"That's what I said. Groger."

Hassina stood over Sermad's shoulder. "Is there a limit?"

"It says limit four."

Hassina's eyes danced with mischief, recording a trip to Kroger as a priority on her to-do list. She decided to place the letter from Obama aside and address a more pressing issue—food. Food and its purchasing.

Later in the day, after the cooking and cleaning were done, after Hassina treated herself to pomegranate while hiding in the garage, and after Fatima returned home from school, the entire family got into the car and headed to Kroger. During the ride, Niran took her time scrolling through her phone to find a good article about Bernard Kroger, a man born in 1860 in Cincinnati, Ohio. The city was only 263 miles away from Detroit, a four-hour drive that she could take once she got her license.

She stared at the blue, evil-eye, beaded ornament hanging on the rearview window and imagined visiting Bernard's childhood home if it still existed. Kroger's German immigrant family used to live above a dry goods store that his parents owned. In 1873, they had to close their store due to the economic recession, and at the age of thirteen, he began working to help support his family. The fifth of ten children, he ended up using his own money to open his own grocery store, succeeding despite many setbacks and calamities.

Niran imagined she was Kroger, an Iraqi immigrant, making the most of it until she amazed everyone who doubted or undermined her abilities. She was the legend in her story. She would be a modern-day Cinderella, rescued from her dull existence, discovered, rich and famous as a poet. Or a modern-day Enheduanna, living as a Babylonian princess in an all-American city. She would be free.

In the midst of what she knew society considered an infantile fantasy, but which she was convinced was her true reality, she heard a strange roar from afar and wondered who was making that ruckus. *Also, why, and where was she, anyway? What was happening?*

She recognized her mother's voice, demanding that she get her lower-end out of the car. In a moment, she felt like she was coming out of the water and crashing onto the earth she'd left a long time ago. *What was going on? Did she just have an out-of-body experience?* If so, she did not want to return to her body. She preferred to remain outdoors, where it felt moderately warm. Not here, where it felt moderately cold and damp. *Why was it damp?*

"Let's go," said Hassina. "If you move any slower, the chuck roast will be gone."

Where would the chuck roast go, if it could not walk or fly? Niran wondered. *Can it walk, the chuck roast?*

Obligated, she followed the family she called hers, and a few minutes later, they all stood in the meat aisle, each with an empty cart. Hassina ate sunflower seeds with one hand and picked out chuck roast with the other. The rest of them waited for her to examine the chuck roast before placing a total of four in each of their carts.

"I don't understand why we can't just stick to the rules

and buy four chuck roasts instead of playing all these tricks," Niran muttered to Ali.

Hassina heard her despite the low tone. "You want us to pay full-price, so we go broke?"

"We don't have to stock so much food."

"It's not about the food. It's about the sale. Chuck roast hasn't been on sale for a month."

"Well, it's about the food too-" Sermad began.

"Why can't you buy four roasts now, and next time it's on sale, buy it again?" Niran asked Hassina, interrupting her father, agitated and annoyed by their simple mentality.

"And you call yourself smart?" Hassina looked at the ceiling, groaning. "Thanks, Allah, I never got an education."

Ali looked about and saw the customers gawking at them. He was embarrassed by all of this and worried if anyone would make an offensive remark at them. He knew if they did, he'd slam them against the shelves of bread to shut them down instantly.

"You guys are making a scene," he said quietly.

Niran caught sight of a nun in the crowd watching them, her eyes unfriendly.

"I don't know why you guys picked Sterling Heights to live in when you knew that it's mostly Christian Iraqis who live here. Didn't you think we'd stick out like a donkey's ass in a car dealership?"

"We picked it because it's nicknamed 'Little Baghdad,'" Hassina said, without looking up, too busy choosing the chuck roast. This task was not as easy as it looked. The finest cuts were those with bright, white marbling of nice fat throughout the meat, and which were dry and tender to the touch. The trick was picking a second cut of equal or lesser value to get the best value.

"There's another city in Michigan, where Muslim Iraqis live. Dearborn," Niran said. "Why didn't you pick that?"

"Because we knew you'd embarrass us there with your liberal jabber. We wanted to protect the family. We didn't put into account that you'd embarrass us on Vazeboog."

Hassina couldn't believe how little her eldest daughter valued the grocery shopping experience, and felt overwhelmed by the amount of work required to educate her on the art of domesticity. Ever since she could remember, she herself wanted to be a homemaker. That was her dream and purpose in life. She was raised on the saying that "The wise woman builds her house, but the foolish pulls it down with her hands" and loved what a traditional woman had to offer—a warm and lively home that she identified with. This meant clean linens, sparkling kitchen floors and counters, good meals, and well-stocked cabinets and pantries. Yet sadly, she lived in a society and culture where training on matters that dealt with home and being domestic have become a lost art.

Bothered that she'd wasted so much time reflecting, Hassina looked around to see where she'd throw the empty seed shells she had accumulated in her hand. She placed them behind a jar of shrimp sauce and proceeded to rub the palm of her hands together, then waved her team toward the check-out.

"Okay, let's go pay for these, wait in the car for about ten minutes, and come back for a second round."

"You want a second round?" Niran asked. "You do it. I'm divorcing this family!" she yelled with restraint, so the nearby patrons would not hear, and sprinted with her cart out of the meat aisle.

"Divorce us?" Hassina asked. "Is there a law in America that lets kids divorce their family?"

"It's called turning eighteen," Ali said sardonically.

"What do you mean?"

"When you turn eighteen, you can legally move out of your parents' home."

Hassina placed one hand on her chest, the other on her cheek. "Ya Allah! She must be learning this stuff on Vazeboog," she said, as she turned to Sermad. "We must get her married quick!"

Her husband did not respond. He had learned from long ago that the best way to deal with his wife, and marriage in general, was to be neutral, and whenever possible, to run away from conflict. The worst advice he ever heard was to communicate with your spouse. He learned the hard way that communication was a sneaky, spooky phenomenon invented by women to ensure men are forced to listen to a load of trivial complaints, including incredibly mean and made-up accusations. At the end of most communication sessions, the man comes out the loser because, of course, her version of the story is always the correct one and he is a liar.

Before they left Kroger, Sermad turned to Ali and told him not to forget the "Bebsi."

"Babba, it's Pepsi," Ali corrected him.

"That's what I said—Bebsi."

Sermad drove with Hassina in the passenger seat, and Niran, Ali, and Fatima sat together in the back. There was a dull silence, followed by the humid air that the AC could not seep away. This is what they called an "Indian Summer" in Michigan, a term which is over 200 years old, but which has no scientific definition and is generally accepted as a warmer than normal stretch of several days that occurs during October to November.

"Tradition is very important," Hassina started to say. "If we don't hang onto it, and we open our doors carelessly, random ideas will come into our home, use it as a toilet, make a mess, and leave." She turned to the kids in the back. "You want random ideas to use your home like a toilet and make a mess?"

Niran, Ali, and Fatima exchanged looks mutely. Fatima shook her head while the other two remained still.

"We must keep our traditions," Hassina continued. "People can't even tell the difference between Arabs and Indians. They think, 'Hmmm... not black, not white like us, definitely not Asian. Must be one of the brown folks with the hijab and the red dot on the forehead...'" Addressing Niran, she added, "Why don't you want to get married?"

Niran had put on her headphones and crossed her arms. She looked up at her mother and saw her lips move, but the words did not reach her ears. She remembered an article she recently read about toxic parents who overreact and create a scene, use emotional blackmail, make frequent and unreasonable demands, and criticize and compare you—the story of her life. Soon she heard nothing as the voice of Gethen Christine once again entered her realm through the phone, and sang, "I wanna tell you something. Can you stop for a moment and listen? I gotta speak my mind, but with you there's only time, time, time."

Gazing out of the car window, she took in the scenery,

letting herself cool down. Something caught her eye—a beautiful, billboard girl with curly, dark hair, smiling at her unashamedly. Niran gawked at the image as it passed her window, her heart racing. She didn't want to be more attractive or desirable to men or other women. She didn't follow any trends, nor did she want the approval, recognition, or compliments of others. She felt pretty with or without makeup, a fantastic outfit, and accessories. Nevertheless, she wanted the independence the girl in that billboard represented. Yes, that was what she wanted. Independence.

The family entered their kitchen and placed the grocery bags on the counter. The conversation about the suitor followed them like a cat's tail, despite Niran's initial attempts to ignore it and shut it down.

Hassina took out each chuck roast carefully and proudly as if it were a silk blouse. She said to Niran, "All I ask is that you see him."

"Mom, I don't want to talk about this."

"If he didn't have great qualities, I wouldn't push the issue."

Niran stormed out of the kitchen without another word, and went into her bedroom, slamming the door behind her. Her parents, her mother, in particular, viewed everything in a practical sense. Even the union of a bride and groom was seen as a merger of business and family. The wedding was regarded as the start of a relationship rather than the consequence of one. It was a contract, rather than an expression of love. But it wasn't just her mother who held these views.

Although love marriages in the Arab world were on the rise, a majority of them continued to be arranged by parents. With dating considered taboo, how would she ever choose her own spouse?

In her culture, free association with the opposite sex was taboo, dating limited to the educated, urban elite, and casual sex—well, that was unheard of. If it was heard of, it was never talked about—or if it was talked about, it was frowned upon. Discussions on this were rare even among the most liberal crowds. Niran assumed these talks were being hosted, but she did not know by who.

She suddenly felt angry as questions that she couldn't voice filled her head. Why was pre-marital sex tolerated among young boys, but not allowed for girls? Why were men permitted to indulge in everything free and fun, including polygamy, but not women? A man provided food and shelter for his family, true, but in return, his wife had to be entirely submissive to her husband. What kind of a compromise was that? Were married women merely servants and baby-making machines? Was that why families were eager to marry them off at a young age with the intent to increase the birth rate? If women were capable of earning in a contemporary society, why couldn't they enjoy the same amount of freedom as men?

She felt even angrier after thinking about all of this. She lived such a contradictory existence, like the two sides of a coin. On the one hand, she defended her religion and tried to prove to people that they couldn't paint all Muslims with the same brush. On the other hand, she was one of the painters who did just that. The majority of her Muslim family, friends, and relatives were devout and peaceful people. They would never dream of physically hurting anyone, let alone their wives or children. Nonetheless, she couldn't deny the truth that, similar to the Old Testament, the Quran authorized a lot of violence, and for groups who followed their scripture word-for-word, this caused more violence.

Niran studied her face in the mirror—her big, bright eyes, full lips, and her smooth olive complexion. She removed her hijab and dropped it on her bed, feeling a sigh of relief, like a burden was lifted off her shoulders and head. She stroked her hair, curious about this body part that, since the antiquity of religious piety, was considered too intimate to be displayed in the open.

She was taught that women determined their own behavior and fate, and yet the underlying tone of her upbringing revealed a different fact. Where she came from, women were blamed for being harassed, and in many circumstances, they were forced to leave school and marry as soon as they reached puberty. It was not a fair existence.

She recited a poem to the mirror, inspired by no other than Enheduanna:

> Be it known you are lofty as the heaven
> Be it known that you are broad as the earth
> Be it known that I am unshakeable and unyielding
> Be it known that I always stand triumphant
> Be it known that I am a woman

Niran sat on the bed, playing with the hijab in her lap. Her hands were stroking it as much as her hair as she wondered what it would be like to live without it. She grabbed a book and read through it mindlessly while she thought about Enheduanna, the daughter of the great Mesopotamian king Sargon of Akkad and the high priestess of the temple of Inanna, who in later years was known as Ishtar.

Enheduanna held a considerable political and religious role in Ur. She wrote during the rise of the agricultural civilization, when gathering territory and wealth, warfare, and patriarchy were making their marks on the world. She offered a first-person perspective on the last times that women in Western society held religious and civil power. After her father's death, the new ruler of Ur removed her from her position as a high priestess. She turned to the goddess Inanna to regain her position through a poem that mentions her carrying the ritual basket:

> *It was in your service that I first entered the holy temple,*
> *I, Enheduanna, the highest priestess.*
> *I carried the ritual basket,*
> *I chanted your praise.*
> *Now I have been cast out to the place of lepers.*
> *Day comes, and the brightness is hidden around me.*
> *Shadows cover the light, drape it in sandstorms.*
> *My beautiful mouth knows only confusion.*
> *Even my sex is dust.*

Chapter 3

Nisreen Yousif stacked pomegranates in a crystal bowl, grabbed her cup of coffee, sat at the kitchen table, kissed the cross on her necklace, and flipped through a woman's magazine. At forty, she loved dressing in style no matter what time of day. Despite her soft and easygoing ways, one could see the stamp of perfectionism on her face, acquired out of necessity and not because she was born with this quality.

When her husband, Jamal, died of cancer over a decade ago, leaving her a widow with two, elementary-aged children, a boy and a girl, it felt as if the world collapsed on her. She was barely in her thirties, had never been on her own, and she'd wept like never before. She lost the only man she had ever known, and he took along with him the dreams they had together of raising their children, marrying them off, and traveling the world. The loss of those dreams was hard on her too. She ended up having to rely on assistance from the government and her extended family, and she worried nonstop about how she would survive financially. She suffered, learned, and grew.

Over time, she became accustomed to her lot as a widow whose children were now orphans who didn't make Father's Day cards at school. Thankfully, she and her deceased husband had a large, close-knit family that included lots of brothers and uncles who acted as parental figures and provided emotional father-bonding. The children, therefore, accepted their reality soon enough and grew up well-adjusted, smart, dependable, kind, and hard-working. Nisreen knew they wished to have their father with them, and her daughter Mary expressed that truth to her once in a blue moon, but her son Matthew never did.

Mary arrived home with some Chinese takeout and stacks of files. She was greeted enthusiastically by her Shih Tzu named Teddy. Nisreen set her coffee cup on the table and got up.

"Oh, honey, let me help you."

"No, Mom, I got it."

"I'll set the table," she said, and walked to the cupboards. "By the way, your father, God rest his soul—his sister—is coming over today with this one guy. He has to fill out her application for home care, and she needs you to interpret."

She didn't call her children's paternal aunt *ama*, as was the Arab custom, because she liked to remind her children of their father.

"Aunt Labeeba?" Mary asked. "Why does she need an interpreter?"

"You know how your aunt is."

Mary was puzzled and immediately scanned her mental to-do list that kept getting higher and higher.

"What time?" she asked, waving her files. "I'll get caught up with my office work before they come."

"Honey, relax. You need to rest too," Nisreen said.

"I wish. But these cases are so important and…. heartbreaking."

"That refugee resettlement agency works you too hard," Nisreen scolded. "Take a break."

"Mom! I like the work. I really do. Today, this family with three kids came in. The dad is so depressed; he wants to go back to Iraq. Can you believe it? I mean, they're Christian. It's not safe for them there."

Mary's interests in religion and politics began when she was a child, after the 2003 Iraq war. It was when the Chaldeans and Assyrians (Christian Iraqis) became the victim of executions, compulsory displacement, torture, and violence. They were also a target of Islamist groups like al-Qaeda and the Islamic State of Iraq and Syria (ISIS). Her activist mentality was fueled by the idea that her indigenous heritage group risked being close to extinction.

The name "Chaldean" stems from one of the ancient groups that inhabited the region now known as Iraq. In ancient times Chaldea was part of Mesopotamia, known as "the cradle of civilization," where writing, the wheel, and the first cities developed in the south of Iraq around 3500 B.C. For the next 3,000 years, kingdoms rose and fell, empires expanded and contracted, outsiders were conquered and repelled here. In the process, the number of people who made tremendous contributions to civilization greatly diminished in Iraq due to the wars and continuous cycles of genocide over the centuries.

Before the Gulf War in 1991, the Christian Iraqis population came up to one million. By the time of the US-led invasion in 2003, that figure had fallen to about 800,000. The spread of ISIS forces across northern Iraq resulted in widespread displacement of the community. Following the group's takeover of Mosul in June 2014, many Christians fled the city along with other minorities. For the first time in 1600 years, mass was not held in churches in Mosul. ISIS's campaign of destruction of minority cultural and religious heritage also affected Chaldean and Assyrian sites and properties.

Mary had left Iraq as a toddler, so she had no memory of that land or its people. But her father told his children many stories about growing up in Iraq in the 70s and 80s when Saddam ruled. Although they did face some discrimination as Christians and non-Baathists, they didn't worry about getting kidnapped or killed as Saddam didn't tolerate the causal murdering of infidels.

She strongly felt that the Chaldeans constituted a "forgotten exodus," completely unknown and understudied from the academic point of view. Mary saw the pain of the innocent and felt that she must do something to help. This was partly in honor of remembering her father, who had felt frustrated that there was nothing he could do. Given his health condition, there was no time to start the thousand-mile journey. Also, his attitude didn't help.

He thought that only the Superman or Superwoman types and people with plenty of resources like Bill Gates and Warren Buffet could actually make a dent. So instead, he simply tried to cope with the injustice, and her mother felt that this, along with other things he witnessed in Iraq, was what led to his cancer.

Matthew came into the kitchen and checked out the Chinese carryout, the usual favorites—Sichuan chicken, Chow Mein, and fried shrimp with cashew nuts. He was glad to be home in time to eat a carryout dinner while it was still fresh and hot. He owned a cell phone store with his uncle, and worked flexible but also odd hours. Sometimes, when an employee called in sick or couldn't come in for whatever other reason, he was stuck late at work. Sometimes, he ended up running errands that took twice as long as he anticipated. So, he was happy at that moment to be home for dinner with his family.

"Wait until I set the table," Nisreen said.

"Mary, still trying to save everyone?" Matthew asked, by way of greeting her.

"Matthew, that's not nice…" Nisreen began.

"Actually, I am, and nothing is wrong with that," Mary interrupted. "I love helping people."

"But in the end, they're responsible for their own lives," he said. "As you are."

Matthew knew his sister was beautiful and smart, but she could also be annoying with her attitude of "I can find a solution for every problem." Whether intentionally or not, she suppressed one's natural behavior to cater to her version of how things should look. Some issues were worthy of "fixing," such as if a chick was with an abusive guy, then she should advise getting rid of the scumbag.

But other things should be left alone for people to discover on their own, not given long, detailed speeches about what one should and should not do. In his view, even though she was good-hearted, she got some weird pleasure from seeing someone get tense or uncomfortable. It made her feel that she was in a far better place or something.

Mary ignored her brother. Her helping not only honored her father, but it meant being a good Christian. She read her Bible and prayed and served others only for His sake and not her own. In the twelfth verse of the seventh chapter of the Gospel of Matthew in the New Testament, it was written that "whatsoever ye would that men should do to you: do ye even so to them: for this is the law."

She wholeheartedly believed in that and wanted to help others when needed and, sometimes, when not needed too. Additionally, although a woman, she saw herself playing the role of a king, her powers resembling that of Sargon of Akkad, known as Sargon the Great, and chronicled as the first person in recorded history to rule over an empire.

Wanting to expand his powers, Sargon decided to extend his military operations to the southern city-states of Ur and Uruk. He conquered the Sumerian king, Lugalzagesi, and he designated his brilliant daughter, Enheduanna, as high priestess at Ur, at the temple of the moon god, Nanna. This was the most important religious office in the land and always given to someone of royal blood, such as the king's sister or daughter. The position equaled that of a king—even more so since priests and priestesses were mediators between the gods and the people. Sargon made this move to avoid offending the traditional Sumerians, who would view him as wanting to take over for himself both the political and cultic titles of the southern cities.

Enheduanna's job was to make a dynastic marriage with the gods and between the people and the ruler. In this manner, the Semitic Ishtar would be syncretized and united with the Sumerian Inanna. She presided for forty years over the prestigious temple in Ur. Holding the most important religious office in the land, she spread her theological ideas throughout the country, writing hymns for each of the forty-two major temples.

On the other hand, when work piled up and she felt exhausted, Mary wondered the price she had to pay for being one of the few educated individuals in her extended family. Every time an aunt, uncle, cousin, or person claiming to be a cousin or a friend of a cousin, needed interpretation, translation, etcetera, they came to her to take up her free time and space. She never said "No."

Furthermore, accustomed to wanting to please people, if they didn't ask for help, she offered it, and in some instances, regretted having done so. Of course, she never admitted this to anyone, not even to herself.

Chapter 4

Wearing headphones over her hijab and a scarf around her hips, Niran belly danced as she swept the floor. The slight jiggle of her curves added to the meaning of this mundane work, and it was also a time for introspection and a chance to embrace her natural, feminine, hourglass figure. She shook her buttocks and breasts and twisted and rotated her hips in a most alluring manner. She used the broom as her dancing partner and did sensuous lift and drop moves with her hips and shoulders, even spinning and swinging the broom and throwing her leg over it.

Her body relaxed into the rhythm as she rehearsed and imagined what it'd be like to one day dance with her Arabian prince, who also, of course, knew all the best, western dance moves. Although not eager to get married, she didn't want the broom to replace a partner for too long—the thought of having a real partner, someone who was not a father or brother, who was *halal*, lawful, to dance with, was appealing.

Her body movement and beats of the song bathed her spirit with joy and lifted her mood to a state of utter freedom and independence. She could've gone on like this forever had she not suddenly noticed her mother standing nearby, yelling at her. The headphones had silenced Hassina's presence and voice, but Niran couldn't ignore her anymore.

"What?" Niran asked, removing the headphones. "I can't even clean in peace?"

"Don't forget to boil the cabbage and onions in the garage, so it doesn't stink up the house."

"Yes, sergeant!" Niran said, making the salute of a soldier.

Hassina reached for her sandal, and Niran ducked.

"Shit," she said, as she narrowly avoided it.

Hassina didn't stop to aim again. She had other things to do. They went their separate ways, and Niran continued cleaning while also swerving and shimmying to the beat of an Arabic song.

She was cleaning the toilet when the house trembled with the all-too-familiar, over-the-top slam of the front door. Niran stopped and peeked through the window. To her horror, she saw her mother trot across the street with a letter in her hand. She was walking up to Mary, who was retrieving mail from her curbside mailbox.

"La hawla walla quwwata illah billah!" Niran said in a panic, slapping her right cheek. "Don't tell her we're on food stamps. Ya Allah!"

Thinking it was best not to leave the matter completely in God's hand, Niran left her cleaning tools and quickly walked across the street to Mary's house as well. As she approached them, she heard Mary tell her mother, "Auntie, it says they're cutting off your food stamps."

The silence that followed was so thick that you could peel the skin off of it as if it were an orange.

"What? It can't be," Hassina said. "Why would Obama bring us here if he didn't plan to feed us? Might as well have kept us in Iraq to get bombed away. Makes no sense. Please, read it again."

Mary scanned the letter again, shook her head, and

returned the letter to Hassina. "Auntie, I'm sorry, but that's what it says."

"They can't do that!" Hassina said. "We've gone through hell and back, war after war after war, and now Obama wants to starve us?"

Niran felt like she had arrived at the scene just in time to rescue their family's name from further embarrassment, or at least attempt to.

"Mom! No one is going to starve," she said.

Hassina ignored Niran and asked Mary, "What's the phone number to the White House?"

"I… I don't know…"

"Can you look it up for me on Vazeboog? Please, Allah bless you, your mother, and brother. May Allah look after your deceased father. May Allah send you a handsome and wealthy husband."

"I'll look into it," Mary said.

Hassina waved the letter up at the sky, at Allah, and left. Niran and Mary were left alone outside, and Niran avoided eye contact.

"It says that you didn't submit the re-certification form," Mary said.

"What re-cert-ifi-cat-ion form?" Niran asked, pronouncing the word with difficulty.

"About 45 days before the end of your certification period, your caseworker sends you a re-certification form. You need to complete that and send it back."

"Oh."

"I help refugees fill out these applications online. I can do that for you too," Mary offered.

"No, thanks," Niran said, feeling insulted. "We'll handle it."

Niran strode back to her house. The garage door was open. From within the bowels of the house, Hassina ranted unintelligibly. Niran ignored the ranting and headed to the stove to fulfill her chores of boiling cabbage and onions. The cleaning task that she had abandoned would have to be put on hold for now.

She boiled the vegetables and then transferred them from the cooking pot into a serving bowl. She then lugged the pot outside and dumped the hot water on the grass. Looking across the street, she saw Matthew, who stood next to his car with a box in his arms. He returned her gaze. Rattled, she broke her stare, quickly returned to the garage, and put the pot on the stove again. When she looked back out, Matthew was gone, and so was his car.

Suddenly, her mother's rants seemed to rage at full volume from inside the house. Niran jumped at the sound and looked behind her. In a panic, Ali ran from inside the house into the garage, looking for a place to hide.

"What's wrong with Mom?" he asked Niran, when he saw her.

"We didn't fill out some form so the government, or in her words, Obama, will personally cut off our food stamps," Niran explained.

"Oh shit."

"Yeah, welcome to World War III."

"So, we lost our food stamps, and it wasn't because I found a job," Ali said with relief.

"Maybe Mom will let us both get jobs now."

"What do you need a job for? You're going to get married."

"Idiot! Give me liberty or give me death."

Ali sat on the couch, grabbed a handful of sunflower seeds, tossed them in his mouth, cracked them with his teeth, and spat out the shells on the floor. Niran grimaced as she looked at him.

"And a job will give you liberty?" he asked.

"A job with some dignity and significance, sure," Niran replied after thinking about it. "Certainly not a job at a fast-food joint that hires only the weak and the not-so-bright."

"How'd you find out about the food stamps?"

"Ms. Mary read us a letter that Mom got."

"Mary?" he asked, his face beaming.

Niran got up, grabbed a broom and dustpan, and dropped them on Ali's lap, indicating to him that he should clean up the shells of the sunflower seeds. However, he moved them to the side.

"Yes, Mary. You and mom's favorite person."

"Do you think Mary would ever give me a chance?" Ali asked with a grin.

"Are you fucking crazy?" she snapped at him. "She's as conservative a Christian as they come."

"Some Christian girls date Muslim guys," he said nonchalantly. "Besides, I'm an atheist."

"Are you high? You want to commit suicide?"

"Funny how before we came to America, our parents told us that we could have whatever we want here," Ali said. "But every time I want something, I'm given a reason why I shouldn't have it. You can't get a good-paying job because we're on government assistance. You can't get the girl you like because we have a different religion. You can't flirt because some girls find it offensive. And the list just goes on and on."

"I know what you mean," Niran said, sighing and considering her list of dos and don'ts, which were a lot longer than her brother's.

Muslim women were not allowed to marry a non-Muslim man or disobey a husband. Interaction with the opposite sex was not permitted, though some, or actually many, Muslims broke this rule. Wearing tight clothing, showing cleavage, piling on perfume and makeup, or making long or strong eye contact with men was forbidden as it drew attention and caused improper sexual feelings for men.

A Muslim woman was not allowed to pray, read the Quran, fast, or have sex during her menstruation and of course, having pre-marital sex was the most taboo of the rules! If they were "true" Muslims, they definitely wouldn't go outside without a hijab—or that was what her mother and other women relatives thought and strongly felt.

The yelling from inside the house got louder.

"Man, when do you think it's safe to go back inside?" asked Ali listlessly.

"I don't know, but I'll play it safe and chill out here until tomorrow," Niran said, and examined the garage. "Wouldn't be so bad. My own little hut where I can write all night long and dream of another world."

"You're too wrapped up in religion to dream, Ms. Jewish, slash Christian, slash Muslim. All your religions are stolen," Ali said, as he launched into his tirade. "Judaism is stolen from Sumerians, Christianity is stolen from Egyptians, and Islam is stolen from Zoroastrian, which is Persian."

"They're your religions too," Niran insisted.

"I'm an atheist, remember?" he replied with that grin again.

"Good for you. I pour holy water on the ugly child," she gestured, pretending to do so over his head.

"Niran, when are you gonna start wrapping the grape leaves?" Hassina yelled from the inside.

"Knew it was too good to be true," Niran said with a sigh.

"When is that dolma getting cooked?" Ali asked.

"Sunday, as usual. This family is always thinking about its stomach."

Ali got up to go inside, disappointed that each time he craved dolma, this famous Iraqi dish of stuffed vegetables like grape leaves, onions, cabbage, zucchini, eggplants, tomatoes, or whatever other vegetable could be stuffed, had to be dangled in front of him like a carrot.

"Do you think there's real freedom anywhere?" Niran asked him.

"Not sure," he said. "They say it's here. We'll have to find out if that's true."

He went inside, and Niran moved the cabbage to the side and inspected her reflection in the tray. She pulled a few hair strands from her headscarf and posed in different directions, slowly embracing the beauty of her sex appeal and charisma. But she didn't remain there for too long, afraid to wake up the footloose and fancy-free woman that lived inside of her. Instead, she stopped looking at her reflection, and grabbed a notebook and a pen from the table. She sat down to write to her heart's delight, where her true identity felt safe and protected, where her words flowed through like a waterfall. Moments later she stopped, and wondered, *What if someone reads this?*

Another moment passed, and she decided that she would

most likely destroy these papers soon. She would shred and recycle the results. She put pen on paper, and the words flowed as she wrote:

I want to remove the hijab. Wearing it is an act of patriarchal subjugation, a form of modesty imposed by men because they do not want to take responsibility for their stupid arousal. Personal accountability, people!

There is so much hypocrisy, with men and women trying to "interpret" the will of Allah instead of following it. A true Muslim is not defined by her hijab, but by her virtues. Having said all that, where would I find the courage to do what I want to do?

I still live with my parents, who believe the hijab is obligated by Allah Almighty. The Lord, and even all scientists, agree to this, they say! They'll say that the hijab is a form of worship like praying and fasting. But who cares what they say? I care more about the Creator than the creatures that came up with these absurd laws.

True, my family will be angry and lash out at first. They'll say terribly hurtful things—Mom especially. They might even banish me, but with time, they will get used to it. Won't they?

She stopped writing as she considered what to write next. This was complicated and not merely a matter of standing up against the tide. It required proper planning, some serious evaluation of her circumstances, and fear, a good amount of fear. Diversion of Islamic laws, in even the smallest degree, could bring harsh consequences. She ran the risk of hurting the people she loved, including harming her younger sister's future marriage prospects, causing her parents to become outcasts, and cutting off some, if not all, social ties. The issue was also a question of belief, of mixed feelings on her part.

Did this mean stepping away from her religion, eventually not even identifying as a Muslim? Was she committing a sin and making a pact with Shaytan by taking off the hijab? Would she end up in hell for it?

Niran suddenly felt so disillusioned by religion and its countless, bizarre rules that she became nauseous. She wanted to remove the hijab without the drama of having to be labeled as a nonconformist or a rebel. All she wanted was for her gender to be valued, for her feelings to be treated with respect, and to walk freely down the street without people making assumptions about her. She wanted her strong spirit and her brave soul to shine so that she could be ready to accomplish the bigger dreams in her life. That is all she wanted.

Putting on her headphones, Niran searched for a rhythm on her phone, a song that could easily move and inspire her. She searched and searched and decided she would once again listen to Gethen Christine, to her incredible voice and moving words. Although they never met, Niran felt they were kindred spirits. Gethen conveyed a persona that mirrored Niran's personality; she evidently depended on social media to reach her audience, but she deserved more recognition, a larger following, and was waiting to be discovered.

Gethen posed these questions in her lyrics:

What kind of life do I want?
What kind of life have I always dreamed of?
What kind of person have I always known of… inside? Inside.
There is a life out there that I want.
There are these dreams I have to live.
No matter what choices I have made in the past,
I am me, my being, the one that still lives…

Once Niran finished listening to the song, she began to whisper her own mantra before returning inside the house.

I am a rebel child.
My body, my voice!
Don't tell me what to cover.
Or what to leave exposed.
Don't tell me what I need.
Or how to wear my clothes.

Chapter 5

With Teddy beside her, Mary sat on the cluttered bed. There was paperwork scattered around her, along with some new and old women's magazines. Her bedroom was dominated by the color pink and decorated with floral printed pillows, light-colored paintings, and other feminine décor. There were a lot of makeup and perfumes on the dresser.

Occasionally, she glanced at her reflection in the mirror and saw a beautiful girl, but she saw one who lacked the power to express herself. When she talked, she thought that she sounded boring and wondered whether this was the reason why men couldn't connect with her. They admired her beauty, yes, but treated her with either disdain or immaturity.

Her mother advised her to be patient and wait for Mr. Right. Mary knew that was the right answer and the right thing to do, but it felt so wrong. It seemed that the rest of the girls who were her age were enjoying a different lifestyle, one that she didn't want or really have access to.

Was she too mature for her age, given that her father passed away when she was a child, and she had to grow up to the reality of life too quickly? She had to begin worrying about her mother and her brother from an early age. She even worried about her dog and worried about her father. She often wondered, *Where did my father go, and was he happy there?*

Was she too religious, and therefore, caught up in the

church's long list of unnecessary taboos? As a believer, has she shut her mind too tight in fear of bringing onto herself moral harm that compromised her human conscience? While she would never verbally admit to this, in her deepest, darkest secret hours, she questioned if there were speckles of falsehood in scripture, and if there were, will one day parishioners point them out to their congregation so that she too might build a backbone and speak up?

The sound of the doorbell pulled her away from her contemplation. However, she stayed on the bed until she heard her mother calling for her to open the door. She got up, went to the entryway, and opened the door to find her Aunt Labeeba standing there, a plump woman in her sixties.

Leaning against her cane, she tottered and let out a lot of "Ahhs!" and "Oohs!" appearing to be in apparent pain. Beside her was a stranger, a man in his seventies who was tall, skinny, and hunchbacked. He wore old glasses, old clothes and held an old briefcase. Mary turned on the front porch light as she welcomed the guests.

"Good evening, Auntie," she said warmly.

"I'm Mike. I need information," the man said.

Mary thought it was a strange introduction, but said, "Sure. Come on in."

Teddy appeared and barked at the intruders. Aunt Labeeba dropped the cane and hid behind Mary in fear.

"Qaddisha Allaha," she prayed in Chaldean Aramaic. "Miriam wa Mshiha!"

"Auntie, it'll be fine. He doesn't bite," Mary said reassuringly.

Nisreen came from the kitchen and hurriedly took Teddy away. Relieved, Labeeba straightened her clothes and gratefully kissed and hugged Mary. Mary, Labeeba, and Mike then moved to the kitchen, where they sat around the table.

"Tea? Coffee?" Nisreen asked.

"Tea, thanks," Mike said and cleared his throat. "I just need information."

"Tell him I can't walk," Labeeba said to Mary, continuing in the Aramaic language.

"What did she say?" Mike asked.

"It's Chaldean, or Aramaic, or a Chaldean dialect of Aramaic," Mary said to Mike, flustered, wondering if she'd tried too hard to explain and therefore looked guilty of something or another. Then she looked at her aunt.

"Auntie, you just walked into our home," Mary told her.

"You call that walking?" Labeeba continued in her native language. "It was more like crawling."

"What did she say?" Mike persisted.

"She's asking what kind of information do you need," Mary said.

"She has Medicaid?" Mike asked.

"Yes," Mary answered.

"She gets Social Security?"

"Yes."

"She gets food stamps?"

"Yes."

"Oy Gevalt! She's getting the whole caboodle. What more does she want?" Mike exclaimed.

Labeeba used her fingers to count: one, two, three, and four. Mary nodded to say that she understood.

"She wants home care," Mary said.

"Can she cook?" Mike asked.

"No."

"Can she bathe alone?"

"No."

"Can she take her medicine?"

Mary asked her aunt in Aramaic, "Can you take your medicine?"

Labeeba shook her head and mumbled her answer to Mary.

"A family member has to be there to read the prescription," Mary told Mike. "Otherwise, she'll mix them up."

"Alta kaka, kvetch!" Mike cried with a sigh, unable to bear this old-timer, first-class complainer.

"What did he say?" Labeeba asked Mary.

"What did she say?" Mike asked Mary, then quickly added, "Can she dress herself?"

"Not without assistance," Mary answered.

"So, she can't do nothing," he said, taking notes. "Oy vey! Oy vey! Oy vey!"

"What did he say?" Labeeba asked in English, and catching herself, she covered her mouth.

Mary shrugged and asked Mike, "What language are you speaking?"

"Mucho vici es fakakta!" he said, ignoring Mary's question and then continued in English, "You'll have to get papers from the doctor about her health—or lack of. I'll send the forms to you. Write down, she can't do nothin'."

Shortly afterward, Mike dashed out of their home in a way that resembled someone escaping a prison. Mary stood at the door, waving goodbye and hoping this meeting wasn't too damning. When she went inside, she saw her aunt tying her hair in a bun, removing her shoes, pulling up her sleeves, and speaking in perfect American idioms. There were no more "Ahhs!" or "Oohs!" She even tried to help Nisreen cook by saying, "Sis, let me do that."

Nisreen waved her off, but with a flip of her hip, Labeeba nudged Nisreen away, grabbed a knife, and chopped the onions.

"What are sisters for?" she asked.

Mary, who tried to be as good and clean as humanly possible, watched the façade melt away with conflicting feelings. She was an accomplice in helping another individual commit a crime, if this was a crime and not merely a misdemeanor. But even if it was a mere misdemeanor, in God's eyes, wasn't it still a sin? Or, was it automatically forgiven since this was an elderly person, her aunt, to top it off, her father's sister?

She decided to ignore her righteous attitude, quickly un-process the information she took in, and use laughter as a mechanism to wash away any immoral activity she was involved in by going on Facebook. After posting some biblical quotes on her page to demonstrate she was holier than thou, she scrolled through her family and friend's pages to see the idiotic, low-quality, comical, and plain stupid things they posted about on it.

Chapter 6

Niran wore her gym shoes, placed her headphones over her ears, and walked to the living room where her mother and father sat in front of the television, watching an Arabic soap opera. Her mother was in tears as she watched the show, but she was also frantically cracking sunflower seeds and throwing the shells on the floor.

Niran briefly glanced in their direction, and couldn't help but think, *the world is full of people who sit in front of their TV and do nothing productive with their lives.* But she didn't say that out loud. Instead, she said, "I'm going for a walk." She was promptly ignored by them and headed out the door without another word.

Niran walked vigorously on the sidewalk. It was dark and quiet, the perfect atmosphere to practice a Facebook Live post. This time she chose to record directly to the iPhone's camera first. Consequently, she couldn't see where she was going, but more importantly, she got to recite her poetry.

When the morning dawns
I will climb down from the pomegranate tree
and begin my journey to the moon
where I will lay upon its little mounds
covered beneath seven quilts
and think about my dreams…

Her thoughts came crashing down by a sudden impact against a chest that didn't have the functional glands that women possessed. She screamed, and her phone tumbled to the ground. It was Matthew, Mary's brother.

In the dark, they went on their hands and knees grappling for her phone, its screen still shining, and the camera still recording. As they both tried to grab the phone, their hands intertwined. Niran nervously pulled hers away, protecting them like a lioness, and simultaneously, afraid of the warmth emanating from him that felt similar to the breath of a dragon. Even though she had never felt the breath of a dragon.

He picked up the phone, and they both stood up. As he offered Niran her phone, he accidentally brushed his forearm and hand against her chest, causing an electric spark on her skin. The sexual bells and whistles caused a ferocious, death-like rage.

She seized the phone, turned off the recording, and ran away. Matthew stood on the corner alone, watching every morsel of her silhouette, deeply affected by her guarded behavior. If she wanted to rip him into pieces, he thought, he'd happily let her. Maybe he could send her that invitation.

Niran rushed inside her home's open garage, feeling breathless. Ali was sitting on the couch, watching her gasp as she came in. Without a word, she pushed a button, and the garage door closed. She paced back and forth like a newly caught jungle animal placed in a cage.

"What's wrong with you?" Ali asked.

"I just ran into Mary's brother," she said.

"So?"

"Why the hell is he out walking at night?"

"Why the hell are you out walking at night?" Ali retorted.

"I've never seen him out walking before. It's weird."

"You think he's stalking you?" Ali asked with some concern.

"No, but I hate the way he came out of nowhere. What are the odds of that and when… I was…" Niran stomped her feet. "God, I'm so annoyed!"

"Why? What happened?"

"I thought no one was out, so I was rehearsing for Facebook Live."

Ali laughed gleefully. "He basically saw you make a fool of yourself?"

"It's not funny," she whined. "I'm already embarrassed enough with that food stamp letter that Mom showed Mary."

"Do Facebook Warriors shit in their pants when someone sees them posting crap?" Ali asked, while laughing. Niran ignored him.

"I hope Mary didn't tell her brother about the food stamps," she said.

"They seem like a nice family. Why do you care what he thinks, anyway?"

"I have no privacy."

"Facebook Warrior Seeks Privacy," Ali said, mocking Niran with a fake headline.

She didn't respond. She was suddenly not sure about anything. Of course, she would never admit to it. Sometimes, it felt good to be strong and unique, complex, and sophisticated. Sometimes, she hated the thought of having different skin and wished to paint herself all white. Or switch her personality as easily as one switched the light bulbs on and off.

She should write a book about her life and give it the title *Apple Chicken Nuggets*—something that didn't make sense, but sounded tasty nonetheless. *What a crazy idea! How do I come up with such silly things?*

She went into her room and grabbed her notebook. She fiddled around for a few minutes before she began to draw a radish, a black radish. She searched for information about black radishes through her phone and discovered that there was such a vegetable. It belonged to the family Brassicaceae and was a variety of winter radish, also called Black Spanish radish.

There were dozens of recipes available for it, which included buttered black radishes, black radish chips, black radish with truffle oil and caramelize, roasted black radishes, a Mandarin, Napa, and black radish salad, pickled black radish, and even black radish potato salad.

She scrolled through the recipes and then stopped. Her fingers hesitantly changed the phone screen to access the camera. Fear swept over her as she stared blankly at the 43-second recording of the incident between her and Matthew. *But what was the fear?*

"Oh, go away," she begged of her thoughts, not wanting them to open the door to questions that would identify the joy she felt when his masculine body bumped into hers.

But why would she not want to open that door, she who is so philosophical, alive to the idea of revolutionizing old traditions? Well, for one thing, she knew she wouldn't feel fulfilled by love. What she was after was a freer expression of self, and yet, something was missing. After all, she was still a young woman, and as a young woman, she had a desire to feel desired.

Startled by her thoughts, she put her phone away and lay on her back. The moment she closed her eyes, her conflicting thoughts disappeared. All the noise was instantly replaced by the delicious memory of her body colliding with Matthew's.

Hassina and Sermad finished their evening prayer, stood up, and folded their prayer rugs. Hassina moved to the kitchen, and Sermad turned on the Arabic Channel. Fatima did her homework on the floor, and Niran sat on the couch, reading.

"Mom, I have to write something nice about Dad," said Fatima.

"For what?" Sermad asked.

"For a homework assignment," Fatima replied.

"So, what do you want from us?" Hassina asked.

"To write something about you."

"So write it," Hassina said matter-of-factly.

"I don't know what to write."

"What are you going to school for?"

"Babba, you have to help too!" Fatima said after seeing that she wouldn't be getting any help from her mother.

"Go ahead. Ask me questions."

Fatima shuffled through her schoolbag and brought out a paper. "What is the most important thing you ever taught us?" she asked.

"I don't know, Babba," he said. "You're supposed to know. Ask your sister."

"He taught us to be honest and to stay out of trouble," Niran said.

"It has to be at least two paragraphs," Fatima said. "That's two words."

"It's actually two sentences," Niran corrected her.

"One," Fatima said.

"Please don't be such a pest right now," Niran said. "Go, go—leave me alone."

"I will not! You have to help me with my homework. All the other kids get help from their parents."

"Come here, Mamma," Hassina said, motioning for her youngest. "What do you need?"

Fatima snuggled beside her mother. "Mamma, what is Babba good for?"

"Nothing. I'm the one who put this family together and made us who we are today. Write that in there."

Ali walked in the front door waving the mail. He dropped it on the island. Niran noticed from afar the Secretary of State label on one of the envelopes so she grabbed it and tore it open. She took out a durable, flexible plastic card which looked like an actual driver's license, with her photo, personal information, and the state seal.

"I got my driver's permit!"

"God help us," Hassina grumbled.

Niran jumped up and down, screaming, while Hassina opened her arms wide and prayed ardently. Rather than feeling annoyed by her mother's "even when I'm wrong, I'm right" attitude, she embraced her. She kissed and hugged her and thought her to be the most wonderful Arab mother in the universe, even though she butchered brand names with pride, used her sandal as a weapon, called her children cows and donkeys when they misbehaved, and pronounced things however she saw fit.

"Babba, when are you going to take me out on a drive?" she asked.

Hassina flipped through the rest of the mail, not responding to the hugs and kisses.

"Niran, stop acting strange. See what this is. Maybe another letter from Obama," she said, as she tore the envelope and handed it to Niran.

Niran dutifully opened the letter and read it. "It says you won a cruise ship!"

Sermad turned off the television and came into the kitchen. "Will it fit into our driveway?" he asked.

"I mean, a cruise trip," Niran said a bit sheepishly.

He and his wife looked over Niran's shoulder at each other.

"What are the dates?" he asked.

"Hold on, Babba," Niran said. "Sometimes, these things are a trick to get you to buy something."

"No trip, no popcorn," Sermad said. "Tell them anytime in January is good. Or after—remember your cousin's wedding is in December. You know what, make it February, when it's cold in Michigan. That way, it'll feel like a real fuckation to sit out there in the sun…"

"Babba, how many times have I told you—vacation—with a V?" Niran corrected him.

"That's what I said. Fuckation."

Niran rolled her eyes, and read the letter before she said, "We have to call them for details."

"Get her the phone!" Hassina demanded of Ali.

Ali brought Niran her phone, and Niran made the call.

"What's happening?" Hassina asked.

"It's just music."

The family hovered over the kitchen island. The scents of allspice, saffron, and curry from the day's earlier meal filled their hearts and nostrils, and a steam of cardamom-flavored tea danced toward them from the kettle on the stove. They inhaled the spirit of this slight gathering, which made them feel that nothing was too bad to deal with, too difficult to achieve, or too sad to endure as long as they had each other.

They had, after all, survived the wars that were supposedly the result of a direct command from God, but more truthfully were intended to divide people, Iraq being as easy to cut into sections as a seamstress cutting a fabric with scissors. Their family longed for better days, where Sunnis and Shias had stable relations, lived together and married each other, where various ethnic and religious groups coexisted. They longed for the nice Iraq that lived in their grandparents' hearts when they recited stories.

Together, they waited.

"Put it on speaker," Ali said, and Niran obliged.

The waiting music swept her imagination, giving her a glimpse of how this vacation could actually become a reality. She started imagining—while her father ate and slept all day, her mother packed the complimentary items, and Ali took thousands of pictures and tried to find ways to party and talk to hot-looking girls, she would lay by the pool, thinking and overthinking, as she formulated words into poetry. On a massive cruise ship, her creativity would soar. She'd be surrounded by the open, unbelievably beautiful sea, and get to experience occasional stops at the most stunning beaches with the whitest sand, bluest sea and…

The sound of a cheerful woman woke her up. "Thank you for calling the Bahamas for a complimentary two-night, three-day Bahamas cruise. Wow, this is really exciting! Your complimentary trip includes unlimited meals in the ship's four spectacular restaurants. Can I have your first name, please?"

The pressure, excitement, red-faces, and heavy breathing in the family circle caused Niran to be tongue-tied, and Hassina had to nudge her to respond.

"Niran," she said, startled.

"Hello, Neewan. How are you today?"

"It's Niran... with an R in the middle... Oh, never mind. It's fine."

"Before we start, are you at least eighteen years of age?"

"Yes."

"Excellent! You've reached our promotion 'Take the Nation on a Vacation.' When was the last time you went on a cruise?"

"Never!" Hassina interjected. "My husband never took me nowhere."

"Sorry, that's my mom," Niran said. "I have you on speaker."

"Oh, not a problem," said the cruise woman, with a burst of pretentious laughter. "This offer is available exclusively to our first 500 callers."

"Thank Allah, and me, that we called right away," said Hassina.

"One question," Sermad said. "When do we go? My brother's daughter is getting married in December, you know."

"You have eighteen months to travel."

Sermad smiled with relief, the cruise trip coming back to life for him.

"Sounds great, right?" asked the cruise lady. "You're excited?"

Everyone nodded their head as if they were in a classroom and wanted to prove to their teacher they were attentive and active in class.

"Included in the trip is a free two-night, three-day stay at our four-star resort in Florida, where you can enjoy three white-sand beaches, four spectacular pools, five exciting water slides, two serene waterfalls, one swim-up bar, and three catered meals."

"What's for lunch?" Sermad asked.

"Can we bring the kids?" Hassina asked.

"I'm not sure what the lunch is, sir, but the cruise ship includes breakfast, lunch, and dinner at large, banquet-style restaurants. Now, this offer is good for up to two people. Any additional persons and you have to pay an extra fee."

"Oh, good, we're two," Hassina said.

"How is that?" Sermad asked. "We're five."

"Don't count the kids," she replied. "That's how it is in this country. Kids eat free."

"Ma'am, I'm afraid it is limited to two persons, regardless of age," said the cruise lady.

"I thought people under eighteen don't count in this country," Hassina said.

"The kids are not kids, Hassina," Sermad said.

Hassina reflected. Their children were as large or larger in size than the average adult, but as useless as a diet soda. They would sit and watch her juggle the whole world and never lend a hand. If she asked for one tiny favor, they behaved rude and obnoxious. It seemed that they never wanted to grow up.

"Great," the cruise lady jumped in. "Now, what credit card do you use? Visa, MasterCard, or Discover?"

"Credit card?" Niran asked.

"We have no credit cards," said Hassina. "Not enough work. We are refugees... Been in American for a short time. My husband does not speak English good, and my daughter does not read English good."

"Well, ma'am, the trip is free, but there are port and tax fees. They're not included."

These words confirmed to Niran that this was a scam, so she prepared to end the call, but Hassina confidently took over the conversation. "No problem," she said. "We can use our food stamp card after they turn it back on. You see, my daughter didn't read a letter that Obama sent us and I had to go to Mary..."

"Food stamp card?" the cruise lady interrupted, sounding pretty surprised.

"Yes, so as I was saying, my genius daughter nearly ruined our lives..."

"Ma'am, I'm afraid we can't use a food stamp card," the cruise lady interrupted once again.

"Why not? Everyone accepts it."

"Yeah, Groger accepts it," Sermad said to support his wife's claim.

"Who?" the lady asked.

"Groger," he said, stupefied by her unfamiliarity.

"I'm sorry, that's our policy. Plus, you have to pay for your own transportation to Florida. But the rest of this fabulous trip is free!"

Everyone was quiet. Wordlessly, Sermad hung up the phone. With a sigh, Hassina smacked the back of Ali's head.

"What's that for?" Ali asked, rubbing his head.

"You can't trust advertisements here," she snapped. "The other day, there was a commercial selling kids. What kind of country does that?"

"And what kind of cruise ship never heard of Groger?" Sermad said.

"Babba, I told you a thousand times—it's Kroger," Niran said, then turned to her mom. "And there's no place in America that sells kids."

"I have seen it with my own eyes," said Hassina. "This one Sears commercial said Three-Day Kids Sale."

At that moment, Niran wanted to do the one thing that was forbidden, or at least impossible to do—to put a lock on her door and isolate herself for months from the people she loved fiercely and would defend to the death, though it was not easy. Their backward thinking and primitive ways suffocated, even embarrassed her. They chattered loud in public places, accepted every possible complementary food and drinks, only read Kroger ads, still didn't know how to properly use a remote control or iPhone, and worse of all, never tried to improve themselves.

She wanted to isolate herself with her other half, the poet goddess queen of the night. She wanted to be an exceptional woman, for her writing to express the human condition in a way that changed people's lives and to affect tremendous change in politics, religion, and literature. Even if she wasn't outwardly successful, her writing would be worth reading. The impact of it on those who followed her would lift them to greater heights which they'd never experience otherwise. Like Enheduanna, her life's work would one day be taught in schools.

Chapter 7

Iraqi Forces Have Taken Control Of Several Districts In
Eastern Mosul, The Military Said.

Trump Shocks Media And Destroys Narrative, Says He
Needs God's Wisdom.

Melania Trump Wants To Focus On Stopping Cyber
Bullying As First Lady.

Bill's Former Lover Bombshell: "Hillary Had Multiple
Abortions, Is A Lesbian."

Hillary Clinton Shared Her Tricks For Not Letting Donald
Trump Get In Her Head, And We Can All Learn From It.

The FBI Has Launched An Internal Investigation Into Its
Own Twitter Accounts.

Niran scrolled through Twitter, but didn't get too involved emotionally. Today, all she could think of was her driver's license and the possibilities it offered. When she heard the front door open and close, she rushed out of the garage. She saw her father in his car, starting the engine, and rushed to the driver's car window.

"Babba, when can you go with me so I can drive?" she asked eagerly.

"Ahh... Well, I usually don't get home until after dark,"

he said, avoiding eye contact with her. "I don't want you to practice at night."

"So, what does that mean?"

"We'll talk about it when I get home. What's the hurry anyway?"

"I can't do anything without a license. I can't register for college and I can't get a job."

"What do you need a job and college for?" he asked, nervously. "A beautiful girl like yourself?"

"Babba!" she said, fuming.

"I'm real sorry honey," he said. "Your mother has been getting on my case, threatening me and… okay, okay. The next time I get a day off, we'll spend half of it driving."

Niran pouted as he backed the car out of the driveway and drove away. Sermad watched his daughter through the rearview mirror and felt guilty that he could not attend to all his children's needs and wants. In Iraq, society placed a lot less pressure on what the ideal family should look like. If you had food on the table, a roof over your head, a steady job, and plenty of love to go around, you had it made. In America, expenses never end and hard work didn't equal success. On top of everything, you had to worry about your son and daughters hanging out with the wrong friends and getting into serious trouble. Disheartened, Sermad shook these forlorn thoughts away and focused on the road while listening to an Arabic radio station.

The next day, Niran paced back and forth in front of her dad who slept on the couch. The room felt claustrophobic, with her body yearning to ride a horse or a bull or a lion and as if competing in a race, maybe even a rodeo. Hassina finished her prayers and rolled the rug up.

"Stop hanging over your dad's head," she said. "We have a million things to do."

"He's supposed to take me driving," said Niran.

"Let the poor man rest," said Hassina. "What's the hurry?"

Niran didn't know the answer to that, but she knew that she wanted to reach somewhere, to find her special purpose in life. She was not meant to live a relaxed and cool lifestyle, to sit idly and simply survive on drink, food, and sleep.

> *O house sent from heaven*
> *visible from my room.*
> *Shrine of white glowing*
> *hearts and castles,*
> *you shine like the moon.*

The day moved along heavily and Niran felt sluggish as if a massive mound rested on her shoulders. She cleaned and paced the house some more, and eventually, she found herself in the open garage again. Discouraged, she stirred the pot of cucumber stew with one hand and wrote in her journal with the other hand. She wrote about a prince, the lord of the faithful word, who lights up the horizon and shines on heaven's vault and… She saw Matthew coming. The pen stopped in its tracks.

He sauntered up the driveway and stopped at the garage entrance. They gazed at each other and felt an everlasting abundance of emotions. Time stood still as if they were on the banks of a river with raging, dark waters, afraid to speak. Finally, Niran smiled, signaling for him to declare the purpose behind his visit.

"Ah, my sister wants to help you fill out the letter, er … the application for food, ah … food stamps online," Matthew said, the words food stamps scratching his throat like a dull razor blade.

Those words ruined her poetic and romantic mood, and realizing she shouldn't be so friendly, Niran composed herself and frowned. She knew the rules; she knew that man oppresses woman.

"Why didn't she come herself?" she asked.

"Sometimes, she's lazy," Matthew said jokingly.

Niran's expression softened and her heart beat with a sudden boldness that rushed through her. She had a request, and she was going to risk it all to ask it.

"Can you do me a favor?" she asked with unexpected courage.

"Sure," he said quickly before she withdrew such an audacious and voluptuous request.

Feeling an intense exhilaration and liberation, Niran drove. She was also frightened by the stormy wind of emotions rising inside her. She felt like she was astride a mythical lion, with her inner voice lifting high and loud like it was singing a song to the goddess.

Matthew sat grimly in the passenger's seat with one of his hands tightly gripping the steering wheel. For Niran, everything was new. She didn't know where to grip the wheel, especially with Matthew's hand in the way. Should she place her hand over his right hand, or on top of his? Should she place it next to his, or at the bottom or top of the wheel?

"You have to signal before you turn," Matthew said.

"People don't really do that," she said naively.

"Actually, they do," Matthew corrected her. "That's why there's order in the streets."

She stared relentlessly into the rearview mirror. He squeezed her arm, trying to bring her attention back to the road, but his touch made her skin burn, not with heat but some strange and powerful sensation. She tried to move it away before she caused an accident.

"Keep your eyes on the road," he said.

She almost hit the curb and screamed. Luckily, he straightened the wheel just in time. He then touched the blue rosary hanging on his rearview mirror, kissed the tip of his fingers, and made the cross.

"Did you take lessons for your permit or did you just pay for it?" he asked, curious.

"What do you mean?"

"You know, pay so you don't get tested?"

She looked at him in shock. "Like a bribe?"

He nodded with an awkward smile, knowing he had said something belligerent.

"Is my driving that bad?" she asked, her feelings of liberation lost now, sunk to the level of the gutters.

She stared at him with confusion; he clearly did not see her as a lady astride a mythical lion, a goddess in disguise. She had given him too much credit for being smart and intuitive, and she had no one but herself to blame for that.

"Well, no, but-" he began, but had to cut off. "Niran, keep your eyes on the road. Slow down!"

Niran parked her analytical thoughts in the back of her mind and Matthew's car haphazardly in his driveway with a jerk. She handed him the keys, thanked him, exited the car, and crossed the street with a great sense of pride and accomplishment. She couldn't wait to reflect on her adventure in her sanctuary. She felt as if the cosmos had ordained that freedom would be her heart's desire, and they had conspired to make it come true.

As she walked away, Matthew scrutinized her, feeling torn. Before now, he only thought her physically attractive and wanted to make a good impression around her. When they were together in the car, however, he had that butterfly feeling in his stomach that he heard people in love talk about. It suddenly dawned on him that he was falling for her.

Niran walked into the kitchen and saw her mother cooking. She hoped the unusual rush of blood going through her didn't reveal the happy excitement she experienced from driving with Matthew. She took great measures to reduce the blood flow, or at least refrigerate it for an hour.

"Where were you?" asked Hassina.

Niran hesitated, feeling guilty all of a sudden, which was a relief. *Perhaps, like ice, the guilt will disguise or smooth out the excitement.* "I went for a walk."

"You took a long time. I got worried," Hassina said, without looking up from her cooking.

"I was talking to Matthew," Niran said, as she poured water into a mop bucket to get started with her chores. Surely, telling half-a-truth was less formidable than telling a complete lie.

Hassina stopped what she was doing and eyed her with

a worried expression. Seeing her mother's concern, Niran explained, "He says Mary will help fill out the food stamp application."

"Allah bless her!" Hassina looked up with joy and opened her arms wide in a prayer.

Niran delighted in having turned an ordinary day into a heavenly sinful pie. She mopped the floor with a rag, the old-fashioned way in the downward-facing-dog yoga posture which nowadays people spent a lot of money to practice in yoga studios. A stranger watching her, the neighbor, let us suppose, would think she was performing ballet, so graceful were her movements.

Hassina opened the refrigerator, which was so packed that several items fell out. She juggled the food and brought out some green beans. In a flash an idea occurred to her, an epiphany. She could use the top shelf of the clothes closets to store some of the items that didn't require refrigeration: the jars of pickles, fruits with hard seeds, peanut butter, garlic, hot sauces, and the ketchup and mustard which could last up to a month at room temperature.

Ali walked in, distracting her new plan.

"What's for dinner?" he asked, sniffing the air hungrily.

"*Timan wa marga*," Hassina said, biting her fingernail, as she considered how else to make this refrigerator and the one in the garage less crowded.

"When are you cooking the dolma?"

"Tomorrow, Sunday."

"Why Sunday if you can cook it now?" he asked, not in the mood for the staple Iraqi dish of rice and a casserole of various vegetables and meats.

Hassina dropped the green beans in frustration. She

never saw such silly problems! In Iraq, she would have had children who did their best to obey her.

"What's with you making orders like this is a restaurant?" she asked. "What's next?"

"Actually, I want to talk to you about that."

"About what?"

"My friends are going to a restaurant, and I want to go with them."

"Oh, that's what this is all about?" Hassina asked irritably. "You're going left and right, up and down—oh, why you cook the dolma Sunday, oh, why not today –going in circles, so you go to a restaurant."

"I've wanted to go for a week, and every time, you say, '*Inshallah*,' which basically means no. I'm going today. I don't care, even if you don't give me the money." Ali was firm, but nervous.

"It has come to this?" Hassina looked up dramatically and threw her arms up. "Allah, what have I done wrong in my life to deserve this?"

"Mom, it's just a restaurant," he said. "Everyone goes."

Hassina removed one sandal and raised it in the air. She'd had enough of this mischievous behavior and would tolerate no more!

"Iskut, ibn al kalb! And you dare talk back?" She waved the sandal threateningly at Ali.

"You brought us here, said we'd live in heaven. Where's this heaven if you can't even go to a restaurant? I can't even flirt with girls without a big fuss," he said, as he walked away, cursing beneath his breath, fervently wishing he could ask his mother, *Do you realize that by calling me a son of a dog, you are implying that you and Babba are dogs?*

"We're about to starve, and all he thinks about are restaurants and girls," Hassina yelled. "Allah, give me patience and give it to me right now!"

"Mom, he's right..." Niran began.

"Don't you start!" Hassina growled, then grabbed the hamsa and spun it in the air to ward off the evil spirits that kept finding a way to sneak into the house. All of the sudden she paused as something caught her attention. She walked to the washed dishes stacked beside the sink and caressed the rim of a plate while sighing heavily.

"Remember, Niran? Remember the china that we had in the china cabinet?" she asked in an unusually sad voice. "I used to say, don't use these bowls, these spoons, these *istikans*. Save them for the guests. Now we don't have the china anymore, and we're the guests in someone else's land."

"We'll be fine, Mom," Niran said gently as she looked at the *istikans*, small glasses Iraqis drink tea in. "Don't worry."

Hassina sighed some more, fatigue overtaking her. The years of suffering that her family endured as refugees made her a lifeboat in an ocean of chaos. Many nights she had gone to sleep with a sense of a beast devouring their innocence as a bear devours meat.

Horrified, the world watched ISIS destroy several countries, but mostly witnessed through the media the damage done to the Christians, Yazidis, and other minorities. The systematic mass murder of Shias did not receive the same attention because, among other things, it lacked the number of gruesome videos that ISIS regularly sent to the media. Even Sunni tribes suffered at the hands of ISIS militants, aside from their share of persecution after the 2003 war.

To add insult to injury, when the Al Mousawi family

became refugees, no Arab country was willing to take them in. They all shut their doors to Iraqi and Syrian refugees while the western countries welcomed them with open arms. That was when she learned that it was humanity one searches for in times of need, not religion, or anything else.

Niran closely observed her mother while she was lost in thoughts, and she saw something she didn't often see—a low mood filled with serious pain and much disappointment. In an unusual show of compassion, she hugged her mother tight, and Hassina hugged her back. She took comfort in her mother's special scent of tenderness and bonding that were knitted during her baby years. Hassina didn't wear perfume, but the warm food odor and the sweet smell emanating from her muumuus was better than any fragrance she ever inhaled.

> *Queen, you have come to the highland.*
> *For my sake, you have entered*
> *the rebellious regions,*
> *have not shied away*
> *from my battle,*
> *over which hangs its dreadful trembles.*

Later in the day, Niran stood in the living room and stared out the window at the droplets of rain that started falling over the autumn yellow, red, and orange maple trees. Her father came behind her and affectionately squeezed her shoulders.

"Everything okay, Babba?" he asked.

She turned around and laid her head on his chest,

desperate to once again be that child whose only desire was to please her parents and collect their love.

"Just thinking," she said.

"About what?"

"About Iraq, the family and friends we left behind."

"Yes, we all miss them," he said sadly.

"I think about what ISIS has done to that land. I wish I could go to Iraq and join the army."

"Remember what I taught you? The most powerful weapon is your mind. If you stay alive and you write and speak, you can reach out to more people to influence them. If you die in battle, you're just another casualty. What good does that do?"

"That's what you taught me," Niran said boldly. "And yet, you and Mamma give me no freedom."

"Oh, that's not true…"

"Come on, Babba, don't you hear what Mamma says about the suitors?" Niran said, as she brushed his reassurances aside. "All she cares about is marrying me off."

"You know your Mom is cuckoo. I thought you're smarter than me to listen to her."

Niran laughed and he kissed her forehead.

"I want to fit in here," she said.

"Don't worry. It'll take some time, but it'll happen."

He left her alone to reflect, and she returned her gaze to the window. The droplets of rain had now turned into heavy rain. Her thoughts traveled to her birth country, to that land that seemed to have been fighting nonstop since biblical times. At times she felt sad for its turmoil, and imagined herself on the front line as a freedom fighter to help Nineveh rise again.

Other times, she wanted to protest and shout, "How dare these criminals use as their acronym the name of the goddess Isis to refer to their terrorist state?"

Other times, she believed that land is forever doomed.

In the foyer, Hassina stood in front of the coat closet and stacked on the top shelf food items she had taken out of the refrigerators: the jars of pickles, peanut butter, garlic, hot sauces, fruit, and ketchup and mustard.

Once done, she was quite satisfied with herself, and after she patted her hands against her muumuu, went on to the next vital task. In the kitchen, on the stove, Hassina burned coals in an incense burner. She put incense-soaked wood chips over the hot coals, and smoke swirled into the air from the incense burner. She inhaled the smoke, enjoying the exotic scent and marveling at these chemicals that, when burned, produced a nice scent and held some cleansing magic.

Hassina asked God to protect her and her family from evil spirits, or to at least calm these spirits down. She then walked around the house, twirling her hamsa, chanting prayers, and wafting the smoke of the incense around the house. She was not only thorough but also focused on the most unlikely places—under the couch cushions, in her husband's sock drawer, under the toilet seat, inside the kitchen trash can, and even inside the refrigerator. This brought the incense cleansing to a close when the food fell out of it, despite her having de-cluttered it earlier.

Outside, on the front porch, Hassina threw out the

burnt ashes of the incense, but the wind blew it right back in her face. Begrudgingly, she slapped the dust off her face and her clothes.

With headphones worn over her hijab, Niran walked briskly in her neighborhood and listened to a mesmerizing song by that same female singer as before, that Gethen. Soon, she started to utter delicious poetic words.

> *The light was sweet for her.*
> *Delight was spread over her.*
> *As the light of the rising moon,*
> *She, too, was closed in enchantment.*

A hand tapped Niran's shoulders, causing her to jump in surprise and turn around.

"Sorry," Mary said.

Niran took off her headphones.

"I found the food stamp application online," Mary said. "Come over, and I'll show you how to fill it out."

"Right now?"

"Your mom wouldn't mind, would she?"

"Oh, Mom would not mind me going to Zimbabwe, or the moon, to save her food stamps."

The girls chuckled and Niran followed Mary to her house, but stopped at the curb, observing the Virgin Mary statue and the sign "TRUMP: Make America Great Again." A great storm brewed, laughing in the sea foam, playing in the waves, mighty Lady, what is this country coming to? She calmed her tumultuous mind and just moved forward.

Inside Mary's kitchen, Nisreen sliced a pomegranate on the kitchen counter while Matthew sorted bills at the table. Teddy barked at the appearance of Niran and Mary.

"Hello, Niran," said Nisreen, taken aback by the sight of Niran whom, prior, she had spoken often about with Mary but she had only seen her from a distance. "Come on in, honey. Teddy, hush!"

"Hello, auntie," she said.

"Mom, Niran and I are going to work on their food stamp application in my room," Mary said, then turned to Niran. "Want some snacks and water?"

Niran could barely hear her with Matthew in the room, watching her. She felt the heat from his eyes that made the air in the room boil like a cauldron of soup. Niran thought it best to guard herself against this heat with all her might. Mary nudged Niran, and she slightly came to her senses. She saw Mary was still waiting for the answer to her question.

"Smacks... Uh... I mean snacks, would be fine," Niran managed to say.

Mary grabbed a bag of chips, two bottles of water and led the way down the hall. Niran followed with utmost reluctance, turning this way and that as she unconsciously kept Matthew's attention. She could not ignore the obvious and yet wondered if she was falling into a trap where she thought Matthew had feelings for her. *Was he interested in the pleasure of her company or something else completely?*

They entered Mary's small room, and *Oh, what a sight!* Niran found it to be a major contrast to her plain room. It was dominated by the color pink and decorated with floral-printed pillows, light-colored paintings, and other décor. There were also a variety of makeup and perfumes on the dresser, and various women's magazines scattered on the bed.

Mary, polite and business-like, sat at a small desk. Using her computer, she logged into the food stamp website.

"Sit down," she said, motioning to Niran to sit wherever she liked.

Niran slowly sat on the bed, next to a pile of women's magazines, and examined the room with envy. The pillows on the bed made it look so sumptuous and inviting that she wanted to lay her head down and take a nap. The mixture of fragrances created a mist so thick that she could see the droplets suspended in the air. On the wall was a picture of Jesus with long, loose hair, but no scarf.

Mary cleared off a corner of her desk and gave Niran a small pad of paper and a pen, then pulled a makeup stool next to her desk chair. "Come closer so that you can see what I'm doing," she told Niran. "Here's the information we need, write this down."

Niran sat on the stool to take notes, but she was distracted by everything in the room. On the wall behind Mary's computer was a colorful collage of magazine pictures of glamorous couples hugging and walking hand in hand on beaches. The environment made her feel as though she had entered another realm of existence. In another world, in another lifetime, this could have been her.

"You don't work, do you?" Mary asked.

Niran stared at the romantic collage on the wall and remained motionless.

"Are you looking for a job?" Mary continued, oblivious that Niran was only partially present in the room.

"No, not yet…Oh, sorry…" Niran pulled herself out of her reverie, and she started to take notes.

"Are you looking for a job?" Mary asked again.

"Waiting to get my license. And I want to improve my English."

"Your English is good enough."

"Good enough for what?"

"For… many jobs."

"Such as?"

"Well, McDonald's is hiring."

Niran's eyes widened, insulted at the suggestion, the realm of existence she'd entered into moments ago pulled from under her feet.

"It's down the street, so you can literally walk there, so you don't need a license," said Mary, unaware of the fact that she had hurt Niran's feelings. "I know the manager. She's very nice."

Deeply offended, Niran stood with an abruptness that startled Mary.

"I need to… ah… use the bathroom."

"Oh, sure," Mary said, confused by Niran's sudden request. "It's right outside, to the right."

Niran dashed out, leaving Mary to ponder over her awkward behavior. She locked the bathroom door and took deep breaths before she looked at her face in the mirror. Tears trickled down for a moment before she stifled her sobs and covered her face with the hijab. But then she burst into tears. *McDonald's! What an insult. It's true, Mary thinks my family is dirt*, she thought, as she cried into her hijab. She wished to find something, anything and break it into pieces.

O shrine, your outside is a luxuriant height
Your visible façade touches all people
Binding the land in a single path
A mighty river, opening wide its mouth
Gathering widespread cosmic powers.
At your root is great terror.

Niran eventually stopped crying and took some more deep breaths. She looked in the mirror and saw that her face was now puffy and her eyes were red. Frantically, she searched for something around her and saw makeup on the counter. Her mind reeled, but she was determined to erase the insult and walk out, looking as if she was not at all affected by it. She flushed the toilet, turned on the water, cooled her face by splashing water on it, and dried her eyes and face with toilet paper.

Wide-eyed and reticent, she carefully used Mary's puff to powder her face. She reached for the lipstick, rolled it up and saw it was pink. Very carefully, she patted the tip on her lips, ever so slightly, then squeezed her lips together and used her finger to spread the color. Looking about, she picked up a perfume atomizer, studied it, sniffed it, and aimed it at her neck before squeezing the bulb.

Oh, no! Too much! she thought in panic. She grabbed more toilet paper and tried to wipe it off her. Closing her eyes, she breathed in the scent until she felt better. Opening her eyes, she adjusted her hijab and beamed at herself in the mirror. She hastily wiped off the lipstick with some toilet paper.

Niran opened the bathroom door, stepped into the narrow hallway, and immediately bumped into Matthew.

She gasped in surprise and the sudden, close proximity between them. Matthew did not attempt to move away. There was less than an inch between them. Their close proximity forced her to notice his well-defined, broad shoulders and the solid chest, his lean forearms, and the nice smell, while he took in her beautiful face and whiffed her perfume. Abashed, she waved her hand to remove the smell.

"Are you okay?" he asked, almost in a whisper.

"I think so," she responded in the same whisper. "Did you tell anyone you took me for a ride?"

"No."

"Good." She waited for a second, and then that same sense of courage she had before reemerged. "Can you take me again?"

"Sure."

"Tomorrow? Around noon?"

"Yeah."

They smiled at each other and then parted.

Niran returned to the room, still frazzled, still put off. Mary, still business-like, studied Niran and frowned. She sniffed the air, noticing something different, but unable to identify it. Niran lowered her gaze, anxious to sprint out of this house at once.

"I better go home," Niran said. "It's getting late."

"But, we haven't even started," Mary said, holding a list. She saw in Niran's impatient eyes that she wouldn't be able to convince her to stay, so she gave in. "Here, I added to the list you started. This is the information we need. Come back tomorrow? I get home by about six."

Niran took the list.

"Okay," she said grudgingly. She clutched the doorknob to make a quick exit.

"Wait," Mary said.

She handed Niran one of the magazines. Niran just stared at it.

"Read the articles. They'll help your English."

Niran looked at it as if it was a dangerous thing, but then she took it, thanked Mary, and left. She ran across the street to her house, where she hurried into her room and leaned against the closed door. She pressed the woman's magazine against her chest and smiled. A loud knocking followed.

"Niran, where have you been?" Hassina demanded. "Open this door!"

Niran hid the magazine in haste and opened the door. Hassina poked her head in and sniffed loudly.

"I went to Mary's house."

"What?!"

"She needed me to help her fill out the food stamp application," she said, knowing the words "food stamps" lulled her mother into a state of tranquility.

"Oh, well. That's great news."

"Yes, it is. Now goodnight."

Niran quickly closed the door, but Hassina wasn't done yet. More knocking followed and Niran had no choice but to open the door again.

"What's that smell?" Hassina asked.

"Oh, that's, ah … it's Bebsi."

Hassina wanted to say more, but Niran closed the door on her, and broke out into uncontrollable but silent laughter. Once she collected herself, she grabbed her journal, laid on her bed, and began to write.

Pomegranate

You prince, the pure-handed,
Priest of Inanna
Heaven's holy one, full of silence.
His thick and beautiful hair falls down his back.
He has built his house on your radiant site
and placed his seat upon your dais.

Chapter 8

Before the night ended, Niran went into her dream world again. The woman's magazine was placed beside her head so that after she fell asleep, she could receive any spiritual messages from her superior. She flipped through the magazine, running her fingers over the shiny hair of the women models and the men that were shown flirting with them. She opened up her laptop and placed her fingers on the keyboard, but then swiftly removed them.

She pushed the laptop away, stood up, and paced in the room, eventually stopping in front of the mirror to check her headscarf—the mirror that conveyed her cosmic vision and moral distress.

In the ominous dream,
the ominous dream of what
the nightly vision brought me,
I do not understand.
Let me take my dream to my father
and may my dream-interpretress,
an expert in her specialty,
reveal the heart of the dream to me.

She took a selfie, sat down on her bed and began to untie her hijab, dropping it into her lap. She picked up her pen and journal from the bookshelf beside her bed, along with a book of endless Sumerian songs and literature. She set the book on her pillow, cracked it open, and left it there to bathe her abode with petals. Opening a new page in her journal, she began to write her deepest desire about the prince of pure delight who came joyously out of the bright sky.

> *Youth greet the prince with the stars' hearts,*
> *a jubilant moonlight, and abundant light.*
> *Gift him with a house on the earth,*
> *where the queen will take him in with compassion,*
> *and the king will prepare the ceremony*
> *for his passage into manhood.*
> *The girl awaiting him will cover her back with wool,*
> *looking like a stately lamb,*
> *her bed sautéed with the aromas of sensuousness,*
> *unable to sleep*
> *as she anticipates the prince with loving devotion.*

She took a deep breath and took another selfie. She then sat down, and nudging her journal aside, typed on her laptop. "Have you ever considered removing your hijab?" She read the question out loud as she typed. "Be honest. I have."

She made some revisions, reviewed her remarks several times through a subsequent, semi-blurred vision, too excited and nervous to clearly see what she was doing. Before doubts crept in and sabotaged her courage, she posted these three sentences on Facebook, and smiled. The shells around her, made up of the path that her family had carved for her, began to crack. She was now feeling a writer's bliss in the territory of the large insurgent mountains and she desired to nurture it daily with milk and bread so it could grow to a billion published words.

Lounging on the bed with the laptop on her lap and the woman's magazine, the Sumerian book of songs and literature, and her journal beside her, she watched the screen with a blend of joy and fear. Within minutes, comments began to tumble in like oranges falling off large crates. She was beginning to feel anxious to grab each orange, peel its skin, eat it and feed a few bites to the mountain inside her.

"Last week, a haji died defending your hijab and you want to remove it? Allah first!" One Facebook user, a so-called friend, posted in their comment.

"It's a matter of choice and wearing a hijab doesn't make you pious," Niran typed in response.

"Enjoy yourself now, but wallah, we'll laugh at you on the Day of Judgment," another Facebook user with the username *Chocolate Kufer* commented on her post, Kufer meaning non-believer.

"It doesn't say in the Quran that women must wear a hijab," Niran typed.

"Don't let the devil use you," said a Facebook commenter with the username *Astaghfir Allah*, which is an expression of shame, as if to say, "I should have not done that," and asking for God's forgiveness.

"Thanks, for the advice, bro," Niran typed and posted, unfolding her splendor in the chaos that was being caused in all the lands. But, she was not without her supporters either.

"Good for you!" one random Facebook user wrote. "Now you can wake up and start your day without having to make cultural, religious, and political statements through your closet."

Niran was still looking at her laptop and smiling when the door to her room slammed open with force, and Hassina charged in. Furious and red in the face, she attacked Niran with her sandal at a fast speed that hindered Niran from the opportunity to defend herself. Sermad and Ali rushed in behind her, trying to stop her. Together, they were bringing in a whole whirlwind of muddled feelings that were voiced with loud shouts and screaming from everyone.

Sermad finally got Hassina under control and separated her from Niran. Hassina tore at her muumuu, still in anguish and distressed as Sermad pulled her floundering body out of the room.

Once alone in the room with Niran, Ali turned to her and asked, "What happened?"

Unable to respond, Niran just snatched her phone and ran from her room. She rushed out the front door, slamming it shut behind her. Out in the street, she ran, and ran, and ran, not allowing herself to be still and feel the mix of emotions going through her. She ran down the street into the darkness until she could no longer run. Once she stopped, she saw she was engulfed in darkness. Alone here, she shook with grief, the tears of uselessness and unworthiness, anger and fear pouring down her face. The list of negative labels went on and on in her head.

O my Lord, this is my dream
which I've told you about a thousand times.
There was a single, young woman from your land.
She was high as the heaven and as broad as the earth.
They tried to drown her in a great river,
a river of false historians.

O my Lord, this is my dream
which I've told you about a thousand times.
There was a single, young woman from your land.
She was high as the heaven and as broad as the earth,
confidently set at the base of a wall.
Birth her to her highest potential once again!

Hassina restlessly and angrily spun the hamsa in the air, as she paced around the house. Sermad told her to stop and sit down and she listened but she still felt irritated.

"It's your fault!" she said, furious. "You spoiled her. Made her think she can do whatever she wants."

"Relax."

"Like the saying goes, behind every problem is a short girl."

"What?" Sermad asked, utterly confused.

"My honorable family name is on the brink of ruin and you don't care!"

"Let's be honest, Hassina," he said with a tired sigh. "Your name wasn't so honorable to begin with…"

"What?"

"Remember that story about you and the barber?"

"That was a rumor!" Hassina shrieked.

"And what about the falafel kiosk guy?"

"How dare you try to shame me?"

"I'm not trying to do that, but you were no saint, and I didn't listen to these stories because…"

"Because they were rumors!"

"No," Sermad said, looking her firmly in the eyes. "Because I loved you."

Hassina's mood softened and an image of the last time her husband had wrapped his arms around her thick body penetrated through the misery that was inspired by Niran's actions. She calmed down and grumbled to herself, "Taking off the hijab. I'd rather take off my clothes before I take off my hijab."

Sermad wanted to say something to bring his wife to her senses and make her use her head at the moment, but instead, he viewed her plump body and remembered the last time his hands touched her generous, pleasant curves.

The house was pitch dark when Niran decided to sneak back in. Silently, trying not to make much sound, she changed into her pajamas in the dark. She still felt close to tears as she slipped into bed. She placed her laptop on her lap and opened it. The glare of the screen illuminated her face and the tears in her eyes. She was glad to be in the darkness in her room so that no one could see, not even the stars and the moon. She went on Facebook, found and then deleted her original post.

She shut her laptop, grabbed her phone and her journal, and then pulled the covers up over her head. Concealed by the bed covers, still in tears, she turned on her phone's flashlight and started to write in her journal. Quietly in a low voice, she spoke, and wrote:

> *I am a woman. I am loud and proud.*
> *Not to the church or mosque.*
> *Not to the state.*
> *I am a woman, and I choose my fate.*

She paused for a bit as she looked into the phone camera and composed her thoughts. She picked up the pen again and continued to write.

> *They don't know why I wear a hijab,*
> *think I'm wearing it for attention.*
> *They don't know why I no longer*
> *want to wear the hijab. They think it's*
> *only for attention. But I'm not*
> *doing a performance or a show.*
> *What I want is in my heart and soul.*

Fatima tiptoed into the room and came to the bed. She pulled the covers down from over Niran. Niran smiled to her and put her journal and phone aside.

"Come here, little cantaloupe," she said, as she made room for her.

Fatima got into bed with her sister and Niran pulled the covers over both of them.

"Why are there tears in your eyes?" Niran asked her.

"I'm just wondering if life is real or it is a dream," Fatima said.

"Why would that make you sad?" Niran asked after some thought.

"It doesn't make me sad. I just can't figure out the answer—if it's real or a dream."

"Maybe it's both," Niran said, as she hugged her sister close. She kissed Fatima's forehead and wiped her tears. "Don't worry about me. I'll be fine."

"Why was Mom so upset?"

"Because we ran out of macaroni," she said earnestly.

Fatima's eyes widened in confusion, and then she cracked into laughter. The light-heartedness reduced her sadness, and she added, "Only someone who died and came back to life can answer this question—who is the real God."

Niran frowned. "What? Who told you that?"

"It just makes sense. If they worshipped a goat God, it would only make sense for goats to go there, right."

Niran smiled, kissed Fatima again and hugged her even tighter. "Interesting concept. Now close your eyes and go to sleep. You have school tomorrow."

Fatima closed her eyes as Niran uttered half in a whisper:

I am a rebel child!
My body, my voice!
Don't tell me what to cover
or what to leave exposed.
Don't tell me what I need
or how to wear my clothes.

She raised her phone and looked into the camera.

"I miss my birth country," she said in a low voice. "I know I will see it again. Nothing, no borders or religions, will keep us apart."

She put the phone down, closed her eyes, and drifted far away to the land, which once upon a time, not too long ago, she had called home.

Chapter 9

The next day, life went back to its normal routine. Niran regained her composure, having had the opportunity to scream and gnaw the ground enough times the night before. She hurriedly set aside the drama that had taken place between her and her mother and went out to meet Matthew for the second drive that he had promised her.

The moment they met, his presence and the sunshine outside washed away her problems. She was surprised to realize that she felt safe with him. She could post any nonsense on Facebook and he would not judge her for it. They could be out alone in the middle of the night, having a burger in a dark alley, and she would not feel threatened. He had this suaveness about him that said, "If you do or don't want to do something, that's fine. Don't feel pressured to do it out of a sense of duty or responsibility."

Niran was brought out of her reverie by the persistent beeping sound of the car. The seat belt alarm beeped incessantly.

"Don't forget your seat belt," Matthew said.

"Why do I have to wear a seat belt?" Niran asked.

"It's the law."

"Who cares about the law?"

"You don't like laws, huh?" Matthew asked, grinning.

"No. There are too many of them—in schools, in homes, at work, in religion, in governments…" She eyed him before continuing. "Even in love…"

"Well, I'm sorry, but you'll have to put on your seat belt," he said straightforwardly.

"Who's going to make me?"

They stared at each other and a sudden tension appeared in the car. Niran's cheeks started burning and her heart rate went up. To break the awkwardness of the moment and get some oxygen, she said, "Okay, just this time. But only to shut off that damn beeping."

She clicked her seat belt and the beeping stopped. They shared a shy look once again and Niran noticed how happy she felt. The more she got comfortable while driving, the more she allowed herself to go into another world, a world of countless possibilities. She listened to Arabic music that inspired her, evoking emotional feelings in her, making her dance and shake her hips, waist, shoulders, and breasts. This made Matthew rather uncomfortable.

"This isn't a good idea, Niran," he said cautiously. "You need to concentrate on the road."

Treating his advice with trifle, she intensified her moves and asked, teasingly, "What's not a good idea?"

"Belly dancing while you drive."

"This is the best way for me to concentrate. I clean with Arabic music, walk with Arabic music, and write with Arabic music. When I'm deep in thought or pretty pissed off, on the other hand, I listen to American music—to escape."

"Can we at least put on something mellow?" Matthew asked, trying to change the subject.

"Mellow music is dangerous for Arabs, you should know. It makes them super emotional. They either have to be in the happiest of moods while dancing and eating, or they're depressed like they're at a funeral. There's no middle ground for them even though they're called the Middle East."

Matthew laughed.

The day went well, and she was proud of herself. Proud to have driven a car, flirted with a man, showed off her intellectual and quirky discourse, and had fun. Later in the day, she went for a walk. She walked with her headphones over her scarf while listening to an American song. When the song was over, she uttered spoken word poetry to herself as she marched faster and faster.

> *Into my fate-determining temple*
> *I entered for you. I, the en-priestess,*
> *Enheduanna, while I carried the basket,*
> *I struck up the song of jubilations. I now*
> *write up your fate-determining song!*
> *All powerful divinity, suitable for Me and He.*

Her phone rang several times. She looked at the screen and her mother's smiling face appeared with the word "MOM". Niran put the phone on silent and just listened to her own heavy breathing that sounded as if she'd climbed a mountain. She was now running back toward the house. The phone kept vibrating as another call came. She muted it. Then the phone pinged as she got a text. With a sigh, Niran stopped walking. She looked at the text that came in from her mom. It was all in capital letters: *WE'RE GOING TO DIE SOON IF YOU DON'T COME HOME.*

Niran, now at her house, rolled her eyes. She stood motionless for a minute before she headed inside. She wanted to remember the memories of how nice Matthew's attitude was toward her, how kind his words were and the flirtatious exchanges between them. Hearing her mother's voice would ruin the beautiful feelings she was enjoying at the moment and make her mind spin with heavy doses of doubt and guilt. Instead of feeling entranced by the movie-like experience of the car ride, she'd end up being haunted by the idea. It would make her feel like she'd done something wrong and push her to spend the rest of her time justifying it to herself on paper, through her poetry.

She looked up from her phone and saw Mary was waving at her. Instead of going inside, she walked over to Mary's house.

"Did I say something yesterday to upset you?" Mary asked.

Niran avoided looking at her. She didn't want to think about that unpleasant experience either.

"I'd rather not talk about it," she replied curtly.

"Please tell me how I've offended you."

"I'd rather not," Niran said, walking back to her house.

"But you owe me an explanation," Mary called out to her.

Niran stopped walking.

"I owe you?" she asked, surprised and slightly angered by Mary's words. *There's that sense of entitlement again.* Niran was getting extremely annoyed by this odd sense of superiority that Mary exuded every time she talked to her.

"Yes," Mary continued in the same manner. "I helped you with your food stamp application and even suggested work for you, and what do I get? You storming out of my house. Not even a word of thanks."

Niran thought that Mary sounded a bit hurt, which gave her a malicious sense of satisfaction. While she had initially planned just to say sorry and move on, she started to relish the argument.

"There's a lot you don't know about me," Niran said with a stubborn and defensive attitude.

"And you don't know much about me, either," Mary defied her.

"I bet I know more about you than you know about me."

"Oh, what do you know about me?" Mary asked.

"I know that you constantly post prayers on your Facebook page, acting like you're as pure as the Virgin Mary. You act all afraid to touch a guy for fear that you'll get pregnant when in reality, you're pretending to be someone you're not and claiming privilege over anyone who's not like you."

"You stalk me on Facebook?"

"No," Niran corrected her with the attitude of a teacher. "I study you on Facebook."

"Oh, and what did you learn from your studies?" Mary asked sarcastically.

"That you think Obama let people like us come in and destroy your great country, which technically isn't yours," Niran said, letting her annoyance and anger with Mary wash over her. It was like a dam inside her had burst and everything that she hated about Mary was flowing out of her without any hindrances. "You think we're trying to take over and take unfair advantage of U.S. laws to get what we want.

You're one of the many conservative Christians who will be voting for the guy you think is the Messiah who will clean this land of all Muslims."

"Oh wow, I'm flattered you think so highly of me that you've done this much research on me," Mary said in a dead-pan voice.

"You're welcome."

"Can I tell you what I know about you? You, like other moderate Muslims, interpret the Quran the way you want to," Mary said in a calm but cold manner. "Always gloss-ing over more than one hundred disturbing verses that call Muslims to war with non-believers."

"That was allowed in self-defense..."

"Hmmm," Mary interrupted. "And I assume you've also normalized the oppression of women by the fantasy that women living under Islam, somehow, have a more beautiful and exotic life than others."

"You came out here pretending to be the Grand Helper, the Christian Savior when the truth is you wish people like me would disappear."

"I've never said that, nor do I wish that," Mary replied sternly. "Don't make assumptions. That's so immature. I thought you were a better person than that."

"You started it."

"Let's end this pointless argument right now. I'm willing to let this go. Just apologize to me and leave."

Even though she was only a year younger than Mary, in that instant, Niran felt very childish in front of her. Not just that, but she felt stupid as well. She was simply sick and tired of Mary, who always had to come out on top.

"C'mon. You can't give thanks for a favor or say that

you're sorry when you're clearly in the wrong?" Mary asked in a spiteful tone.

As Mary stood there all cool and collected with her hands on her waist, Niran felt an uncontrollable rage build inside her. She could think of nothing other than Mary's sense of superiority suppressing her. All of the sudden, the neighborhood looked vacant and rundown by a plastic covering as the sunshine hid behind the clouds. She felt her face turning red, and tears of anger pricked at her eyes.

"Well, I'm sorry massa!" Niran said, suddenly with a Southern accent and a timid voice, her fingers trembling as she pretended to be frightened of Mary. "I ain't mean to anga ya! I was simply replyin' to you comment! I fogot you was white! Don't whip me massa!"

Mary was stunned into silence. Her mouth hung open as she glared at Niran and wondered if Niran was aware of the gravity of her words and actions. Does she realize the line she just crossed? Could she be that naïve or crude, and if so, which was it?

Niran took Mary's silence as a sign of victory. At last, she had crushed Mary's intellectual garbage, and she didn't care that she had to use low-mannered and merciless blows to do so. Deep down, in the big picture, she won, and that was what really mattered. Hollywood films and major sports games vowed by this win-at-all-cost scheme, so why shouldn't she? Niran nonchalantly put the headphones over her ears and hijab and marched back to her house.

All Mary could do was look at her as Niran disappeared. She fumed to herself while she walked back into her house, where her mother Nisreen sat at the kitchen table, rubbing her temples one minute and the cross on her necklace the next minute. As she often did, she entered the phase of the past, when her husband was alive and their life was whole.

"Matthew, get me an aspirin, please," Nisreen said to Matthew when he walked into the kitchen.

"That girl is so unreasonable," Mary cried. "I want to shake her up and say, 'Look, I would keep debating with your dumbass, but I know it would be a waste of time because you have to be the one with the correct narrative, even though I can outsmart you without even trying.'"

"You're too judgmental," Matthew said to her, his protective instinct toward Niran coming out.

"I'm speaking the truth."

"It might be *your* truth, but it's not *the* truth."

Nisreen sighed, as she rubbed her forehead. Mary noticed her discomfort and grew concerned about the noise level and the subject matter.

"Oh, Mom, I'm sorry. Am I giving you a headache? You're okay?"

"Yes. No. It's not you." Nisreen continued to massage her forehead. "Mary, ever since what happened in Mosul with ISIS, you've become too political."

"You're the one that says 'Arab Jarab'—never deal with Arabs," Mary pointed out. "Now, don't argue with me. You'll make your headache worse."

"Mary, I was including us in the equation too," Nisreen explained. "We keep fighting and playing tug-of-war with each other when we have to learn how to help one another, regardless of religious or ethnic background—Jews, Christians, Muslims, whites, blacks, whatever. We must work together as humans first, or else, we're all doomed." She shrugged her shoulders, then added, "Remember what

Niran's family has been through. War-after-war-after-war. They need help, just like we did when we immigrated. They have the same fears that we once had. They're our neighbors."

"As if I don't know that," Mary griped.

"I'm serious," Nisreen emphasized. "You and Niran are the new generation. You have to do better than what we've done."

Mary tried to come to grips with her mother's wise words, but she couldn't focus. The ranting with Niran continued in her head as she went into her room, and plopped on her bed. If she had not been shut up into silence, she would have confronted Niran about other issues. The way in which Muslims believed their religion was superior to others, which explained their ego, and how they considered westerners immoral who lacked religious values and spirituality.

She would have asked Niran a dozen other controversial questions, and answered them herself. "Did Arabs embrace western cultures? No, they shunned them! In Sicily, they built palaces in the Arab's architectural style, but did Arabs admire any of the Spanish or Italian magnificence or the artwork? No, they shunned, or else, destroyed them! Were Muslims able to question Islam or the Quran without being accused of apostasy or blasphemy? No, they would not dare question, because these were considered crimes punishable by death!"

Seething, Mary took some deep breaths and went on her Facebook account to post biblical quotes about tolerance and acceptance and show that she was on the right path. It might seem hypocritical to an outsider, but it was imperative that she aligned her character and actions with the standard of

Christ's example, even if pretentiously. After all, she ran the race with her eyes on Jesus, the author and finisher of her faith, not the people.

Niran stormed into her house, where Hassina sat at the kitchen table with Sermad. They were cutting pounds of beef into cubes. Hassina was relieved to hear Niran walk in and thanked God for his gratitude. Niran rushed to her room, threw herself on the bed, and grabbed her journal to write in it how she desperately desired to enter a new home, in a new neighborhood, with new people, and a new atmosphere. She was hardly in there for a minute when Ali opened the door. Niran ignored him.

"Mom is wrong for what she did, but why did you go on Facebook and talk about your hijab when you knew it would get back to her?" he asked.

She kept ignoring him.

"C'mon, talk to me," he said.

"Why should I?"

"Because I'm your brother, and I care about you."

After a moment of silence, she answered. "I feel like there's so much inside me that has to be left unsaid because of all the walls around my heart and mind."

"And you want to break the walls through Vazeboog?" Niran laughed.

"You want to lose the hijab?" he asked.

She lowered her eyes.

"You already wear tight clothes, so hey, why not?"

"Gee, thanks."

"It's not in the Quran," Ali said. "You don't have to wear it. The Prophet (PBUH) wanted women to be modest for their protection. If it's putting them in danger, it defeats the whole purpose, doesn't it?"

"I wear it to respect our culture, not for our religion. You know that."

"In this neighborhood, you just bring unwelcome attention to yourself."

"Unwelcome to whom?"

But Ali didn't answer, and Niran noticed that he was looking out of the window. She followed his gaze and saw him watching Mary come out of her house.

"That little prideful peasant," she said sharply.

"Why do you hate her so much?" Ali asked.

She was slow to answer this question.

"I don't hate her."

"Huh!" Ali said with disbelief. "Whenever her name comes up, you get all dramatic."

"You don't understand," Niran defended herself, certain she did not hate Mary. A more appropriate description was that she disliked her. "Yesterday, she told me to work at a McDonald's."

"That upsets you?" Ali asked, genuinely baffled at how that made it okay to hate or even semi-hate someone.

"I feel like … I don't know … like she's trying to transform or convert me or something."

"Well, aren't you the one that wants to change?"

"You really like her, don't you?" Niran asked, wanting to change the subject since evidently she couldn't get Ali to understand how a job flipping burgers did not belong to a poet, a journalist, a modern-day Enheduanna. She felt that because she wore a scarf and was Muslim, words that came out of her mouth were underestimated.

"You think she'll give me a chance?" he asked happily. It was the only thing he wondered about when anyone talked about Mary, but up until now, he had never admitted to that.

"You're definitely a blond. Just shampoo your head, and you'll see."

"You're so judgmental."

"Ali, look. Our immediate family and Mary's are both from Baghdad. Our family is Arab, right?"

"Yeah, and…?"

"Well, we may also have Chaldean blood. When Iraq was invaded by the Arabs centuries ago, a lot of families inter-married. So, we don't know exactly if we're 100 percent Arab, 100 percent Chaldean or a mixture of both. I think we're a mix of both, and that's why I read Sumerian history and like Enheduanna's poetry. But Mary, on the other hand, thinks that because she's a Chaldean Christian that she's not Arab, but 100 percent purebred Chaldean (or Babylonian)—who were the strongest and richest in the ancient-ancient world. She really believes they were the chosen ones…"

"… when both of our lineages might go back all the way to Abraham," Ali said, finishing Niran's sentence.

"Exactly! If we did a family tree, she'd shit in her pants to find that our grannies are probably related," Niran added, feeling glad that Ali could see why she disliked, not hated, Mary.

Before he could reply, though, the door opened, and Hassina looked in.

"We're going to starve because you two won't stop talking about politics and religion," she said, and then she turned to Niran. "Come help me in the kitchen."

She left before Niran could say anything. Both of them looked at the open door in surprise.

"I think she just apologized to you," Ali chuckled.

Later that night, Niran sat on the bed, writing, while Fatima was lying beside her. She thought about the earlier day, and wished that rather than having gotten so upset at Mary, she would have further explained the verses that called Muslims to war with non-believers. Such acts were permitted during a medieval Arabic and Hebrew life and mentality, close to when even biblical stories were filled with this type of punishment for sinners and non-believers. Besides, there were rules not to kill the old people, children, women, preachers, and so on. Furthermore, a study showed that killing and destruction were referenced slightly more often in the Old Testament.

Why didn't Mary bother to look at the beautiful side of the Arab world? The people's respect to their seniors, particularly to parents, their simplicity, and their legendary warm hospitality. Families might be strict, but their closeness, and their loving and caring ways are paramount. A family can consist of over 50 people—parents, children, grandparents, aunts, uncles, cousins, etc.—all having each other's back. They help each other and look out for the welfare of one another, so that no one feels alone or unloved.

Arabs lived a relatively happy and content life as a result to their nearness to God and their acceptance of their holy obligations. In the Quran, *Al-Baqarah*—the Cow—Sura 2, Verse 186, it is written, "I answer the call of the supplicant when he calls on Me, so they should hear My call and believe in Me that they may walk in the right way."

Islam teaches that prayers are answered, both prayers relating to personal matters as well as prayers relating to nations and to mankind. It's a shame how western media sidelined every aspect of her rich culture like poetry, classy music, calligraphy, cinema, and linguistics, and erected a savage image of them.

Her thoughts ranted and ranted until a sudden piercing siren broke the serene silence of the night, followed by blinking red lights that beamed into the room. Niran stumbled out of bed and raced to the window to see what was happening. An ambulance with flashing lights and a blaring siren was parked in front of Mary's house. Niran watched as the paramedics opened the back of the ambulance, pulled out a stretcher, and ran in the direction of Mary's front door. She rushed to tell her family.

In a hurry, Hassina and Niran threw on their jackets, wore their sandals, and crossed the street to Mary's house. They could see two paramedics rolling Nisreen out on a stretcher, followed by Mary and Matthew.

"Daughter, what happened?" Hassina asked Mary.

"I don't know," Mary said, crying. "She said she didn't feel good, and then she got all weak and faint, so I called 911."

Hassina embraced her and hugged her tight. "La hawla wala quwwata illa billah."

Teddy came out of the front door barking, and Hassina screamed as if a wolf had appeared. The situation got chaotic and quickly grew out of control until Mary grabbed Teddy and held him. Hassina wondered why people bothered having live-in pets as she wiped away Mary's tears and continued to comfort her. "La hawla wala quwwata illa billah. I'll cook for you and your brother tomorrow, so you won't starve."

Niran walked behind Matthew toward the ambulance. Discreetly, she placed a supportive hand on his back. Matthew looked behind him, but his focus was pulled back on his mom, who was now being slid into the ambulance on the stretcher. He couldn't bear the sight, and got into the back of the ambulance with her. The doors closed, and the ambulance drove off.

Sitting beside his mother, Matthew's thoughts slipped to his childhood memories of his father. The loss of his father, or rather the realization of it, was traumatic for a boy in sixth grade. At first, he didn't understand, or didn't want to understand, that death meant a person was gone indefinitely. He coaxed himself into believing the separation was temporary and he would see his father soon enough. Some time passed before he grasped that his father's absence was forever, and he began to sob inconsolably. When the dust finally settled, Matthew swore to never forget his father and to always take good care of his mother and sister.

Chapter 10

The street was deserted the next morning when Hassina crossed it. She was holding a large pot in her hand and a Ziploc bag full of food. The hamsa hung from her fingers. Carrying so many items gave her the sense of a professional waitress who balanced multiple plates on her arms. In Hassina's case, she did the job without the support of a brassiere, and therefore, she felt she outperformed a professional waitress.

She went up to Mary's door and rang the doorbell. Teddy barked somewhere in the house, and she fidgeted and prayed. With the lavish flesh around her stomach, thighs, and buttocks, minus the undergarment to elevate her large breasts, running would be painful. Maybe it was best to put the pot down on the porch and leave. When no one came, she began to do just that, but then Mary opened the door.

"Good morning, Auntie," she said in greeting. Her eyes looked puffy and tired.

"Any news about your mother?" Hassina asked. She craned her neck, looking for the dog who was still barking from inside the house.

"She's fine," Mary replied. "Teddy is locked up in my room. He won't come out."

"Oh, thank you. Thank you," Hassina said with visible relief. "Oh, you're truly an angel."

"They did some tests on my mom. I'm going with my brother to the hospital in an hour."

"I woke up early this morning and made you a pot of *kubba hamuth* for lunch. For dinner, you and your brother have to come over."

"Auntie, you really shouldn't have," Mary said with gratitude.

"Nonsense!" Hassina said, smiling. "Just warm it up on medium temperature. Not high, because the meat dumplings will stick to the pot and break apart."

"Auntie, really..."

The dog barked then, causing Hassina to jump a bit and become nervous again. However, she still stayed firmly at the door, pushing the food she had prepared on to Mary.

"We're neighbors, and it's my duty not to let you starve," she said, as she extended the Ziploc bag of food to Mary. "Fried wings for your mom. I know you guys eat American foods as well."

"Oh no..."

"Don't be shy! The food is so bad in hospitals; your poor mother might starve."

"No, really, Auntie. They don't let people bring house food."

"Sneak it in. Put it in your purse."

"She has a restricted diet."

"I can put it in several bags, so the oil doesn't hurt your twenty-dollar purse."

"Auntie, my purse costs 500 dollars," Mary said, with innocent laughter.

Shocked by this detail, Hassina simply waved goodbye and rushed home, her arms supporting her bouncing breasts. She barged into the kitchen, where Sermad sat at the table, flipping through the Kroger ads catalogue. Ali sat next to him, watching videos on his phone. Niran was sweeping the floor.

"Niran! Niran!" Hassina said, breathlessly, while spinning the hamsa in the air. "Forget the *timan wa marga* today. We're cooking more dolma."

"What? Why?" Niran asked. "We just had dolma yesterday."

"What do you mean, what? Why?" Hassina grumbled.

"We normally make it on Thursday and cook it on Sunday."

"Today is a special occasion," Hassina announced. "Mary and Matthew are coming for dinner."

Niran stopped in her tracks. Ali looked up from his phone with his eyes shining. Both of them could not focus on the tasks they had been busy with.

"So, why are we changing dinner then?" Sermad asked.

"I want to serve them something good, and you always say my dolma is the best. You wouldn't believe this," Hassina said in an almost conspiratorial tone, "but Mary owns a 500-dollar purse."

"Mom," Niran interrupted, not wanting to ruin her mood over this detail. "Please, is there any chance that we can eat at the table?"

"Ya Allah, what's the big deal?" Hassina asked. "We're not eating off the floor, we're eating on the floor."

This was an argument that always riled up Hassina. She didn't want her children abandoning their age-old customs of gathering in a circle, sitting comfortably like one did at a picnic because they thought that the western ways were always better. It angered her that her children went to school to learn, but were so stupid when it came to learning about their own roots.

111

If they didn't view her as an illiterate woman who lived in the past and if they didn't disregard her thoughts and feelings, she'd be able to teach them a great deal. The custom of sitting on the floor had roots in every part of the world and was still practiced in many regions like Japan, the Middle East, India, and others. While these localities had been forced to convert to western civilization, they had stubbornly held on to their cultural practices.

The posture was so healthy that it ought to be made the normal way of sitting to do anything. From carrying out tasks, to watching television, to eating a meal, and even for work. The ancient civilizations like Egypt, China, and Mesopotamia created tables to place their objects on, and later, to write, paint, and do some metalwork. However, when it came to eating, it was still a communal affair. Groups of people would sit on the ground, usually on a cloth, and eat food together. The Greeks and Romans made more regular use of tables, particularly for eating, although Greek tables were pretty short and were pushed under a bed after use.

Besides, the purpose of eating together had nothing to do with whether the gathering took place at a kitchen table or on the floor. It was about human interaction and the bonding experience. In fact, it is known that eating together can improve people's bonding. It is said that some friends came to the Holy Prophet (PBUH) with a complaint one day.

"We eat but are not satisfied," they said.

"Perhaps you eat separately?" he asked.

They said that they did eat separately.

"Eat together and mention the name of Allah over your food. It will be blessed for you," he advised.

The Prophet also said, "Eat together and not separately, for the blessing is associated with the company."

Prophet Abraham never ate alone, hastening to seek out company when it came to meal times. If no one was available to share the meal, he searched for a stranger to invite.

Given the historical and religious value that the act of sitting and eating on the floor had, it broke Hassina's heart that her children looked upon this way of eating as a negative thing. Unfortunately, as a woman, and an uneducated one at that, her opinion was not respected.

In another part of the house, Ali stood in front of the mirror, observing himself, posing left and right and checking out all his angles, almost like a parrot. Satisfied, he started straightening his shirt. Then, he made several Arabic signs with his hands to express friendliness, concern, defiance, and outrage. He wanted to try and make it look as natural as possible to make those signs. He repeated the gestures a number of times for emphasis.

Ali sprayed cologne and then coughed as he accidentally inhaled it. He waved his hand to get the mist out of his face. Then he continued to talk to himself. Despite how ridiculous the posturing and gesturing might have looked to an outsider, Ali knew it would change his demeanor, build his confidence and help him be more positive when involved in conversations.

In the room right next to Ali's, Fatima watched Niran stand in front of the mirror, checking herself out, posing left and right to check out all her angles and stroking her hands over her figure. She imitated the poses she had seen in the woman's magazine that was set against the mirror. She picked up her lip gloss and used it again over her already made-up lips. Standing in front of the mirror, she fretted over her appearance. Then she turned to use the perfume and deodorant.

"You already used the deodorant and perfume," Fatima reminded her.

"I did?" Niran asked, a bit flustered.

"Yeah. Why are you overdoing it? Are you in love?"

"No, I'm in the bedroom," Niran joked lamely. Fatima laughed. Niran took a deep breath, and in her heart, she recited a poem.

O city of love,
Set fast upon its platform by the goddess' magic powers.
Built for exorcism, a priestessly craft.
To chant in your house prayers, spells, and charms.
Of heaven and earth,
Deliver me from human nature
By enhancing my qualities and abilities.

Niran had to make an effort to pull her eyes away from the clock. It was nearly time for their guests, the handsome brother and sister duo, to arrive. The family set the dishes on the floor, fretfully and in a hurry. A big fuss was made as Hassina got ready to flip the pot of dolma on a large tray. This had to be done carefully, or otherwise, the tray, pot, and food would come tumbling down. They watched as the layers of colorful stuffed vegetables slid out of the pot.

The doorbell rang, causing dead silence and then a

sudden flurry of activity as they raced to put some last-minute touches on everything around them.

"Babba, can you change your shirt?" Niran asked.

"Why?" Sermad asked, looking at his raggedy T-shirt with genuine perplexity. He usually never wore dress shirts when he was at home.

"You have some nice ones."

The doorbell rang again.

"Who cares what your father is wearing?" Hassina asked, aggravated by everyone's ridiculous concerns. "He's not a model."

"Your mom is right," Sermad said.

Sermad left to answer the door, and Hassina gestured for her children to behave and to put this and that here and there. He returned with Mary and Matthew following behind him. They greeted everyone, and Hassina pointed at the floor.

"We have food all ready for you because you must be starving," she said. "Please sit."

She quickly took Mary's purse and carried it like a baby to the couch. Everyone sat down on the mat on the floor and started passing food around, loading their plates. It was a bit hectic with the cutlery clattering on the plates and the Arabic News Channel blasting.

"Eat, eat!" Hassina continued. "Don't be shy. I made dolma. Everyone loves dolma."

She looked at Sermad. "Lower down the TV's volume. It's so loud that we can't taste the food."

Sermad waved the TV remote, but it didn't respond, so Hassina grabbed it from him and stared daggers at Ali like he was the one at fault. Then she turned off the TV.

"How's your mom doing?" she asked Mary, becoming nice, buttery, and sweet.

"The tests didn't show anything, thank God," Mary replied. "She might come home tomorrow."

Hassina raised her head and opened her hands. "Alif alhumad Allah!" she said, thanking God a thousand times.

The eating commenced. During the meal, little glances bounced from Ali to Mary and from Matthew to Niran. Hassina's and Sermad's lips moved, but their sound was faint compared to the rest of the company. The young people were not paying attention to the adults anymore. The ritual gathering provided fuel for everyone's minds and spirits, creating a feeling of warmth and intoxication. This was one of Hassina's dreams—to have her family and friends over for dinner and share a good time.

Later, everyone gathered in the same circle, sitting and drinking tea in traditional Iraqi istikans. There were plates of palm dates, walnuts, and pita bread. Ali snuck quick glances toward Mary and felt happy to see her. He could never have imagined she would be sitting in his home, sharing a meal with him. Niran snuck quick glances at Matthew. Her feelings were pretty similar to Ali's at the time.

Mary, however, was completely unaware of Ali's feelings. Instead, she studied her istikan with great interest. Then, she said, "My Dad loved drinking tea in these. What's it called, an istikan?"

"Yeah," Niran replied. "The word was brought by the British during the occupation of Iraq and India. They referred to these little cups as an 'East Tea Can.'"

"My dad can do belly tricks with istikans," chipped in Ali, wanting to be a part of the conversation. Niran shot him a glance of wrath while Mary seemed amused.

"No, no...." Sermad waved his hand dismissively.

"Don't embarrass your father," Hassina scolded him while eyeing Niran and Ali. "He has enough problems as it is."

"Come on, Babba, show them what you can do!" Fatima cheered.

Giving in, Sermad leaned backward and placed the istikan on his belly. Then, as he moved his belly, he made it wiggle. Everyone laughed and cheered.

"Niran reads and writes so much, she's like an encyclopedia," Ali added, proud that his last contribution to the conversation had led to such a positive interaction.

"You want to be a writer?" Mary asked Niran.

"More like a rapper," Fatima said.

Niran spat out her tea and blushed with embarrassment.

Sermad fiddled with the remote, but he couldn't make it work. Hassina removed his teacup off his stomach, placed it on a flat surface, took the remote from him, and then turned on the TV. She then gave it back to him. He chose a channel where Arabic politicians brawled, fists flying, and water glasses were thrown at guests—in one instance, even a shoe.

The footage was more dramatic than a purely entertaining wrestling event or tabloid TV show. One man threatened the other to use him to mop the floor. Another said he'd give him a taste of his shoe. It seemed that only Mary and Ali listened to Niran as she continued to talk while everyone else watched and laughed at the TV.

"I used to be shy and timid," Niran said, feeling the need to share her thoughts. "But when ISIS came and did what they did and decided to speak on behalf of all Muslims and to represent me, I was extremely offended, and I got so mad."

"Arab girls are always mad, and they don't know why, and they blame men for it," Ali interrupted. "That's why I don't like to date them."

Hassina smacked the back of his neck. "Arab girls don't date!"

Ali rubbed his neck, which had turned bright red.

Niran rolled her eyes at both her mom and brother, and then went on to explain, "ISIS are terrorists first and foremost. They hate you no matter if you are a Jew, Christian, or Muslim. Unless you adopt their way of life and thinking, then you were considered an infidel."

Hassina's phone rang, and she answered it without looking away from Ali. Her face brightened as she heard who had called her.

"No, no. I'm not busy."

She got up with an extra wiggle, as she sauntered with the phone glued to her ear, toward the kitchen to continue the conversation with some silence and privacy.

"So, I took everything personally and decided to fight too," Niran kept going. "Through speaking and writing. When I talked to people who sided with ISIS, I told them that ISIS misquotes the Quran. Its militants are nothing but uneducated people who are manipulated by political theologies. They have nothing to live for except for the Utopian ideas given to them by others. When I told them these things, I saw people actually changed their minds."

Hassina returned to make an ululation of joy. The call had ended with some good news, apparently. She grabbed the remote from Sermad and turned off the TV. Everyone rotated to face her, wondering what all the fuss was about.

"I have two important announcements," she said with

utter delight. "That was Ahmad's mother. They want to come this week to see Niran."

Niran and Matthew looked at each other, stunned. Hassina pulled out a stack of pictures that were tucked away in her bra, sat down on the floor, and spread the pictures of various men on the rug.

"Mom, this isn't the time, or..." Niran began.

"Hush now, this is the perfect time," Hassina said. "There must be witnesses to see that we gave you options. Otherwise, you'll be crying, 'oh, they forced me." Hassina imitated a child crying, then she picked up one of the pictures and pointed to it. "This is Zuhair. He's standing in front of his house in Baghdad. Look, huge house! Huge! The picture is old, and the house was bombed in the war, but he looks the same."

Niran refused to look at the pictures, and she exchanged distraught glances with Mary and Matthew. Her father watched the drama play out in silence, and her siblings couldn't restrain their laughter as if she was the butt of a joke. Hassina set the picture down and picked up another of a hideous looking man.

"This is Khaled," Hassina said. "Don't judge. Don't judge. He comes from a family that is related to the Holy Prophet, peace be upon him." Hassina put down that picture and picked up another. "This guy has the best mother, I swear. She..."

Hassina babbled on as Niran stood up, wiped her mouth with her blouse, threw an "I'm so sorry" look at Matthew, and said, "Mary. Let's go to my room."

Mary, who was in the middle of drinking some tea, took a last big gulp, put her glass down, nodded, and jumped up. "You bet."

They strode out of the room as Hassina gave them the evil eye and shrugged.

In her room, Niran sat on her bed and gestured to Mary to sit down too. Mary checked out Niran's room and looked around.

"Why do you have two pictures of Jesus?" Mary asked.

"That's Jesus," Niran said, pointing at one, then pointed to the other. "That's Imam Hussein."

"Saddam Hussein?" Mary asked, glaring at the image of Hussein.

"No. No. Eee-mam Hussein, the grandson of Prophet Muhammad, peace be upon him."

"He looks like Jesus."

"He's my inspiration, and I live by his words," Niran said and then quoted him. "'Speak the truth even if your voice shakes.'"

There was silence before Mary inquired. "And why do you have a picture of Jesus?"

"Believe it or not, I'm closer to the Iraqi Christians than I am to Muslims… from other countries at least. At the end of the day, we all eat dolma."

Mary chuckled, and then observed Niran before she spoke to her. "I have never met someone like you."

Mary meant that as a compliment or a tribute, but it took Niran a moment to accept it that way.

"I too never met someone like you," she told Mary.

"You mean that as a compliment?" Mary asked.

"I do. You try to help people."

"It's kind of sad that it took my mom's hospitalization for us to have a decent conversation," Mary said with a sigh.

"Yeah, but it's sad that my mom had to ruin it by embarrassing me just now in front of everyone."

Mary laughed and studied the room some more. She noticed a few hijabs perched on the corner of the bed, one with a purple mosaic print and the other olive with a few lines of glitter. She reached out and lightly touched their fabric. Niran watched her with amusement, but remained silent so not to disturb Mary's apparent meditation. A moment later, she asked, "Do you want to try it on?"

Mary was surprised by this question.

"Come on, just for fun," Niran said. "I'll show you how to wear it." Niran got off the bed, grabbed the hijabs, and held them up. "Which one do you like?"

Mary reflected, and decided to comply with Niran's wishes. She chose the olive-colored hijab, stood in front of the mirror, and said like a cowboy, "Go ahead, teach a Chaldean girl how to wear the hijab."

Niran laughed. "Okay, but I have to do it with you."

Mary was excited to see Niran's hair for the first time, but when Niran removed her hijab, there was a cap underneath it. Niran began to explain, "You have to tie your hair first, and FYI, don't do it when your hair is wet because you might end up with a scalp infection."

Niran handed Mary a form-fitting cap and explained this would help keep the hijab in place. The girls then stood side-by-side in front of the mirror as Niran led the step-by-step process to how to wear a hijab. Mary listened and followed. Drape the long, rectangular scarf over your head with one side longer than the other. Pin up both sides of the scarf under your chin. Flip the longer end of your scarf behind your opposite shoulder. Flip the same end back to the front of the other shoulder.

When all was done, Niran stared at Mary through the mirror, moved by her beauty. "You look so cute."

121

Mary smiled, feasting her eyes on her new look. Niran placed her arm over Mary's shoulders and said, "Think we can pass for sisters?"

"Yes," Mary said without any hesitation.

Niran could not hide her exuberance at the sound of these words. She felt a tribal connection and a better future between her and Mary.

"I'll be right back," Niran said, and exited the room.

Mary further studied herself in the mirror. She had to admit, if it were not for the negative representations linked with this fabric, she would not mind wearing it once in a while for style purposes or on bad hair days. Had it not been mandatory and believed to be ordered by God, with women who refuse to wear it disregarded or shunned by society, and in some instances even faced harm or death, she would respect it entirely. She was all for people making their individual decisions and for enforcing positive praise for cultural differences.

But, in this case, she felt that the hijab was required for discriminatory reasons. Female hair was considered sexually arousing for men and, therefore, needed to be covered in public. Rather than treat their hair phobia, men made it the responsibility of women to be modest and obey. Furthermore, it was not fair to claim that God preferred one gender to dress with certain garments, since no one could prove this claim which in actuality was coercion, plain and simple. After all, didn't God send everyone naked into the world?

Mary sighed and began to untie the hijab. She folded it neatly, and looked at it with compassion and regret, as if it was a baby left at the doorsteps of a convent. The poor thing was lovely and quite fascinating, but it has suffered so much criticism and disdain! She removed the cap on her head, and placed it along with the scarf at the corner of the bed.

She looked around the room some more and noticed Niran's books on the bookshelf. She grabbed the one about Sumerians and flipped through it. She read a paragraph about the Sumerians, how they lived in Sumer, an ancient civilization founded in the Mesopotamian region of the Fertile Crescent, situated between the Tigris and Euphrates rivers. They were known for their innovations in language, governance, architecture and were considered the creators of western civilization.

She was surprised and intrigued by the similarities between her and Niran, and the differences. Niran even went further into Iraq's roots than she herself did. It seemed that she better understood the heart and soul of that region. She returned the book on the shelf and picked up another book. She was not aware that it was Niran's journal. Curious, she opened it and read it.

Layers upon layers of masks
sweep me east and west
south and north
to the point where I can't see
the direction of my path.
I want to remove the masks
covering me from head to toe.

Mary became engrossed in Niran's writing and continued reading. She was still turning pages when Niran walked in and saw what Mary was doing.

"What are you doing?" she asked, extremely upset.

Mary looked up. "Niran, you're an amazing writer!"

"You're reading my private journal?" Niran asked in disbelief.

"I was so in awe with what you told me that I wanted to learn more about you."

"You don't do that by reading someone's journal without permission."

"You're right, and I'm so sorry. I didn't think," Mary agreed as she put the journal down. "I shouldn't have."

"You think you're that privileged that you can do whatever you want?" Niran asked, still angry, feeling vulnerable that Mary had read her journal. *I should've never put my guard down!*

"No. No, not at all!" Mary said, undeterred by Niran's anger, the praises for her work bubbling inside of her. "But you should get your writing published. You have such a strong voice and important things to say."

Niran softened and tried to listen.

"You really think so?" she asked hesitantly.

"Yes, I do!"

"Well, a lot of it is mixed with Enheduanna's, the first writer in history…"

"No. I'm talking about *your* writing. You have to get it out into the world. But first, you must stop hiding behind tradition." Mary paused as she thought and then added, "Behind the veil."

This startled Niran. She fumed and took a step back.

"How dare you tell me to stop hiding when you wear the biggest mask of all? You serve to hide. You act perfect to hide. You hide 24/7."

"I'm sorry," Mary begged, trying to calm down Niran. "Please, don't be upset. But why can't you admit you wear the hijab out of habit, not want? You feel pressured to wear it."

"Or pressured to remove it!"

Ali was silently eavesdropping at Niran's door, and loving the meat of this conversation. None of the Arabic soap operas could provide material as tasty as this. Fatima came up and stood beside him, wanting to enjoy the pleasures of eavesdropping to a good argument.

Hassina caught sight of them both and lifted her leg to grab her sandal. She threw it at Ali, who noticed just in time and ducked while swearing, "Oh shit!" The sandal flew past his head, landing with a thud upon the door. The voices inside stopped immediately. He stood up and straightened his posture and, while he wished to continue to hear snippets of this juicy argument, he knew it was time to end this favorite pastime for now. He opened Niran's door.

"Ah, sorry," he said. "Mom says come eat fruit."

"Tell her we'll eat it in my room," Niran said.

Ali smiled at Mary, then picked up his mother's sandal from the floor, exited, and closed the door behind him, leaving Mary wide-eyed.

"Mary, look, I'm trying to find a way for us to get along," Niran said, attempting to maintain adequate civility so she could get her point across with this prissy girl. "You think I'm hiding behind tradition, and I think... well, I think that your candidate is a hypocrite and so is anyone else who believes that he has any Christian values."

"You're acclimating well with democracy," Mary said, trying to dial it down as well, to use all her powers to be civilized with this savage girl. "You don't like the candidate I support and that makes you dislike me. But that's not logical. Look, I don't like everything about Trump, but I am in favor of way more of his policies than hers."

"Like blocking all Muslims from immigrating here."

"Of course not! I don't want that for you. I'm trying to help you assimilate…"

The door opened and Ali stuck his head in. He did that after having eavesdropped for an additional few minutes.

"Mom says you have to eat the fruit in the kitchen," he said.

"Guess we both have to assimilate to the kitchen," Niran said to Mary. She turned to Ali. "We'll be there in a minute."

He ducked out and closed the door again. Wanting to bridge the gap, Niran grabbed a box from on top of the bookshelf and opened it. She took out a sealed plastic sandwich bag. "This is sand I brought from Iraq."

Mary regarded it tenderly. "Do you miss Iraq?" she asked.

"Yes. Part of me is in that ancient land. And yet, how can I go to a land where creativity is regularly stabbed in the name of religion? Where Muslim clerics come out of the woodwork with the most absurd fatwas, and of course, most fatwas target women. Like girls riding bikes is taboo and women should abstain from purchasing or touching bananas, cucumbers, or any fruit or vegetable that resembles a man's private part."

The girls laughed. Mary considered Niran and the sand, and she regretted having at times treated her insensitively. "How about, let's promise not to argue about politics or religion again—especially not the elections," she said.

"I promise. Besides, why argue about it when she's going to win anyway?"

"Oh, you're sure about that?"

"Yes, I am. I'll bet you anything."

"Okay, let's bet. If he loses, I'll give you a thousand dollars."

"A thousand dollars? If I had that kind of money, you think I'd still be living in this crazy house?"

Mary laughed. "Choose whatever you'd give me if she loses."

"If she loses, I'll tattoo my face."

"With henna or ink tattoo?"

"Ink."

"Honey, you better not make these kinds of bets with anyone, or else your pretty face will get ruined over an election," Mary said, and Niran giggled.

"Niran! Mary!"

They heard Hassina call them from the kitchen.

Niran laughed, and a wind of loud, singing voices came through her spirit and straightened out her will. Suddenly she became determined.

"You know what? If she loses, I'll take off my hijab," Niran said with confidence.

"Yeah, sure. That'll be the day," Mary said, then she stopped to consider. "Well, that's more realistic than tattooing your face."

Ali walked in.

"I know, I know," Niran said, when she saw him. "Come and eat fruit. None of the fruit is shaped indecently, are they?"

"What?" he asked.

The girls chuckled.

"Tell her we're coming," Niran said.

He left.

"So, do we have a bet?" Mary asked.

Niran didn't respond.

"For someone who's so sure she'll win, you have a lot of doubts," Mary teased.

"Alright, deal!" Niran replied with confidence and embraced this positive idea.

Verily, I enter my holy space at your request,
I, the magnificent, I, the Niran,
I carried the ritual basket,
I chanted the Lord's praise
Force lives within me.
It rejects the male ego religions and lies.

Chapter 11

Election Day arrived in all its might and glory. Niran watched the television while she was wiping the kitchen counter. The news broadcasters were talking quickly and passionately, stating their arguments, speculating, and trying to sway public opinion. Their lips were running a race that the viewers could barely keep up with.

They talked faster and faster, and even faster than that. The conduct resembled the auctioneers who chant in a rhythmic monotone, with the right voice, the right speed, and the right expression to lull spectators into a habituated design of call and response, giving buyers a sense of urgency to bid for the items on display. It made Niran's head spin.

She decided to go on her usual walk and to do so at a leisurely pace, with the presence of some pleasant memories. She recalled the recent weekend in Mary's bedroom, when she sat in front of Mary's computer, working on the food stamp application form. This time the experience was completely different from the other one which had left Niran in tears. They had talked, went back and forth with the questions and answers, shuffled through the papers they had, looked up the data field, typed on the keyboard, and checked for data accuracy.

What she remembered the most though, was when Matthew brought in a tray of tea and biscuits, his eyes toying with hers. She had pretended to want him to go away, but inside, her heart was beating loudly for him. It had been very hard not to blush in front of Mary. What she loved the most was that when she went into the narrow hallway, on her way to the bathroom, he was always there. She would have to pass by him, and this was an opportunity for them to chat and flirt with each other.

Her relationship with Mary had evolved into a healthy friendship, which opened Niran's world up a little. Now, Niran felt easy about experimenting with Mary's makeup. Even though she wiped it off afterward, she didn't fret too much when she couldn't get rid of her goofs. Mary always studied Niran's face afterward, and she almost always noticed the makeup, which Niran tried to hide half-heartedly with the stack of papers and by keeping her head down. But in the end, they both laughed at their foolishness.

One day, Mary dug through her drawer and gave Niran a small makeup kit to take home. Niran hugged Mary and this time, it was a true and warm embrace. In the end, after a great deal of work, Mary finally clicked submit. The finished application went into cyberspace, and they high-fived each other. Niran felt empowered by being part of the process rather than resenting having to rely on Mary to provide her with a permanent solution as she would have in the past.

Niran's phone rang, pulling her away from her beautiful memories as she took her walk. She answered, "Hello," without really looking at the screen.

"Come, be terrorist with me," said a heavy and deep voice. It was masculine, and he definitely sounded like he was drunk. "We gonna' drain white America from what they took from us. It's no secret."

"Sorry, I don't know what a terrorist is," Niran said.

"I'm general supa' leader of ground strikes. I'm da general. I run a horse into your living room. Even North Korea fucks with me heavy. Come join me. Where you live?"

"I don't want to participate in harming innocent people," Niran replied curtly, then frowned. "Who are you anyway?"

"Why you actin' all weird an' shit?" he asked, getting irritated, as if he was someone she knew from long ago and should, therefore, recognize his voice. "Dude gave me yo numbe', said you needs a job."

"Who gave you my number?"

"I will get you a job," the man said, ignoring Niran's question. "My war on robotoids is big. We don't harm people. I'm terrorist cuz my powers, baby."

"I'm good, bro."

"You and me," he went on without acknowledging Niran's reply. "We drain these too hip, too cool motherfuckers dry. Say Hadiba."

"What the hell is Hadiba?"

"If you stick wid me, it wid make sense," he said matter-of-factly.

"I'm good, bro."

"What you? No? No... No?"

Niran hung up the phone and walked faster, outraged, but more than that, she felt oddly dirty for having talked to the man. His incoherent ranting made no sense to her, and the malice and surety in his voice scared her. He was so convinced that he was on the right path. She wondered if he was someone who followed her on Facebook and had somehow tracked down her number.

Here in America, I'm nothing but another terrorist! I'm tired of debating and defending myself when I know I've done nothing wrong! Bursting with an unsaid emotion, she stared at her phone and started saying some poetry while looking into the camera.

> *I pray to the everlasting*
> *that this election doesn't take us backwards.*
> *I pray to the everlasting*
> *that in the end, we all stand as*
> *one nation, indivisible,*
> *with justice and liberty for everyone.*

At home, Niran and her mother set the coffee tables with sunflower seeds, snacks, and Middle Eastern salads such as *taboula, fattoush,* and *jajeek.* Fatima lay on the floor, pencil colors and crayons scattered around while she colored in a book. Ali and Sermad sat on the couch and watched the election's early returns.

"I'm going to my room," Niran said, once she was done placing the snacks and salads on the table.

"Aren't you going to watch the elections with us?" Sermad asked.

"Why should I?" Niran asked, with an almost smug smile. "It's such a waste. You know she's going to win."

"You know that for sure?" Ali asked. "You are Allah?"

Hassina gasped and opened her arms wide in horror at what Ali had said. "La hawla wala quwwata illa billah!"

"It's obvious," Niran said, disregarding everyone's opinion.

"A lot of people love him," said Ali.

"A lot more people love her," she argued.

"Go to your room," Hassina said to Niran, already getting fed up with their quarrel and wanting to enjoy eating in peace and quiet. "It's better."

Niran sarcastically gave her mother Trump's two thumbs up and walked out, into the radiant brilliance of her room where she could be herself. Time passed by in a tailored pattern, the way cars pass over the Ambassador Bridge sign, high over the Detroit River on their way from Canada to Detroit. But Niran felt restless in her room. She didn't feel like reading or writing much, and she also didn't want to go watch television with her family.

Impatience stirred inside of her, so she danced it out with grace and arabesque until the stresses and burdens that she was feeling melted off of her. By the time she walked into the living room again with a glass of water in her hand, she felt as light as a feather. She gawked at the television that Sermad, Hassina, and Ali were glued to.

"They're still at it?" she asked.

"He might win," Sermad said, without looking up from the TV. "It's very close."

"It's all for show, you know," Niran said.

"Who knows?" Ali asked. "America is like a woman. You can't understand her. That's why she's so beautiful."

"Hahaha... the only thing I like about Trump is that he's going to deport all these boaters who tell me my hair should or shouldn't be showing. I can't wear my socks with flip flops or..."

"... or eat your peanut butter with pita bread."

Niran smiled, knowing he was joking. "But seriously, he better not win. I bet Mary that I'd tattoo my face if he did."

"Why would you bet something stupid like that?" Hassina asked.

"Because I know he's going to lose," Niran said stubbornly.

"You see?" Hassina asked, turning to Sermad. "And you think your daughter is so smart." She looked up at the ceiling. "Thank God I didn't get an education."

"Mom, I'm going to miss you when Trump is president," said Fatima.

"Why?" Hassina asked, frightened.

"Because he's going to send you back to Iraq."

Everyone burst out laughing.

"Who told you that?" Hassina asked Fatima, while looking at Niran. "Did you tell her that?"

"No, I swear!" Niran said in defense.

"And Clinton is a'pposed to go to jail," Fatima said.

"What?" Hassina screeched. "Who's teaching her this stuff?"

"Mom, everyone at school knows it."

Everyone laughed except Hassina.

Later in the day, Niran caved in. She was now watching the elections with her family and joined them in cracking the sunflower seeds and throwing the shells on the floor. "I feel like I'm going to have an emotional breakdown," she said after a while.

"Slow down with the seeds," Hassina said.

"Allah, bless this country," said Sermad in prayer. "Let's pray that whatever goes down tonight, Allah, protect us from all evil."

"Babba, this is an election, not World War III," said Ali with a grin, but he was taking it just as seriously as Sermad.

"Who's winning?" Fatima asked, trying to make sense

of what everyone was so busy watching. "What are the red colors for? What are the blue colors?"

"You need to go to sleep," Niran said to her. "You have school tomorrow." She looked around, feeling a kind of sickness in the pit of her stomach. She hadn't experienced this since having heard bombs crackling and popping over her rooftop in Iraq. To distract herself, she brought out a nail clipper and started to clip her toenails.

"How many times have I told you, don't clip your toenails at night?" Hassina asked. "It's bad luck."

"And you want me to believe in your Arab superstitions? All these Americans clip their toenails at night and they are living the life while y'all are broke as hell. So, excuse me while I finish clipping my toenails and hopefully join the American bad luck team."

"I want to watch the first, American, woman president win!" Fatima announced.

Niran couldn't fault her for wanting to see history being made, but she feared it might not be the history they'd been hoping for.

"Is there a bucket around here? I think I'm going to throw up," Niran groaned.

Time passed again, turning Niran into an anxious blob of a mess. She slowly carried Fatima to the bed and tucked her in. She peeked out the window and saw Mary's house lights were on. Naturally, she'd be celebrating right now. "It would have been nice for a change to see a woman in the White House," she said to herself.

Bedtime gave Niran no sanctuary that night. She wanted the stars to disappear and be replaced by the sun and clouds. She wanted to forget the idea that it was now too late … too late to imagine that a woman could do the impossible … by becoming the president of this country.

Enheduanna had a similar fate. Her political power and talent in using her poetry to create peace and unity were not appreciated by the people of her land. After her father died, she was exiled from her sacred position, despite the fact that the removal of a high priestess from office was a serious offense. She expressed this injustice through a poem that, through prayer, asked the goddess Inanna to help her regain her position.

It was in your service that I first entered the holy temple,
I, Enheduanna, the highest priestess.
I carried the ritual basket,
I chanted your praise.
Now I have been cast out to the place of lepers.
Day comes and the brightness is hidden around me.
Shadows cover the light, drape it in sandstorms.
My beautiful mouth knows only confusion.
Even my sex is dust.

The sun rose behind the Detroit skyline and the Spirit of Detroit statue. Niran wore the hijab in front of the mirror and afterward, knelt by Fatima's bedside to wake her up. "It's time to go to school, little cantaloupe," she said.

Fatima opened her eyes and asked, drowsily, "Who won? Did she win?"

"No, he won."

Fatima considered her sister's words. "How come a bully gets to be president?"

"Well, honey, this is a democracy, and people vote for who they want."

Fatima was too befuddled and disappointed to respond.

Niran left her house for a brisk walk, badly needing the fresh, cold, morning air. The crisp air that would soothe her broken heart or else lift her away. At the same time, Mary exited her house, crossed the street, and caught up to Niran. They power-walked together on the pavement.

"You're out early today," Mary said.

"I need some fresh air."

Mary smirked. "Are you running away from me because you lost the bet?" she asked playfully.

"No, I'm running away for the sake of running away," Niran joked back, although inside she was in no mood to joke.

"Come on; it can't be that bad."

"Tattooing my face? Oh no, it can't be that bad at all. But I'm going to have to give you a rain check. Sorry," Niran said, as she tried to walk faster and move away from Mary.

"That wasn't the bet," Mary said.

"What?"

"That wasn't the bet."

"Yes, it was."

"You honestly forgot?"

Niran stopped walking to think about what she could have forgotten.

"It was your idea," Mary said to help her remember. "You said that if she lost, you'd take off your hijab."

Niran's face fell as she realized what she had actually

promised. She was also disturbed that she had failed to remember this promise.

"Wow, you, like, blocked it out?" Mary asked, with a laugh. She glanced at her phone and saw the time. "I have to go to work. I'll catch up with you later."

She dashed back to her house, energized by the results of the elections. She considered Trump winning as one of the most important events in US presidential history. It left the majority of Americans dumbfounded and freaking out. The political statisticians who were named the world's most influential people by *Time Magazine* will thrash themselves and weep at their factual probabilities and ludicrous polls, and the Clinton and Bush reigns will burn wrecks on the side of the road. The media will be forever vicious toward those who proved them wrong. Political practices masquerading as the law will crumble the very fabric of the constitution.

Mary prayed that, in the midst of this loud noise and hysteria, Americans would understand the reasons behind Trump's victory. It was vital for them to understand. Otherwise, the country would end up bitterly divided. If they took the time for some deep self-reflecting, they'd see that they were utterly, utterly wrong to judge him the way they did.

Now that he won, she felt that she could be honest and admit that she liked Trump. He was blunt, straightforward, and brutally candid about how he felt about things. If he had a problem with someone, he just came out and said it. He didn't worry about offending anyone. She wished she could do that, say what was on her mind without caring about what other people thought or said about her.

Besides, America was ready for a change. The people desired a president who drove foreign policies like a boss, not a president who felt guilty and apologetic for leading the most powerful country in the world. He strongly believed in a sovereign America negotiating equally and justifiably with other sovereign nations. Trump could end future wars by reversing bad policies that began during the Bush Senior administration. He could destroy the ISIS base, and help Christian Iraqis rebuild their lives in the northern part of Iraq.

Contrary to what people believed, it was not only the "poorly educated" who voted for Trump. Not all people with degrees succumbed to the indoctrination of the globalist, progressive, social justice left. Trump won because voters feared the immoral social trends, including the legalization of Marijuana and possibly other drugs in the future, which might happen with a Democratic administration. Many agreed with his pro-life stance, and they didn't want to become a communist or authoritarian country.

Mary hoped that Niran didn't feel too shocked, discouraged, or betrayed by Trump winning, like the people she saw during the night on television. This was a real-life lesson in democracy.

Once Mary left, Niran started walking again. She didn't get far before she stopped and squatted in the middle of the sidewalk. She thought about Queen Kubaba, the only queen of the Sumerian Kings List. She used to be a tavern keeper, and afterward, reigned peacefully for decades, and was honored as a goddess after her reign finished. Later, however, Mesopotamians decided it was unnatural for a woman to take over traditional men's roles and provided this omen to make sure that no other woman dared to so improperly cross that line again:

If androgyny is born, with both rod and vagina—an omen of Kubaba, who ruled the country. The country of the king shall be ruined.

Ironically, the country of "the king" was ruined because of her absence. The thirst to wipe away the feminine energy, "her story," in the Middle East has succeeded. *It is such that is causing that region to become so imbalanced that, no matter how much U.S. and international intervention, it seems unable to heal.*

Niran feared that this would be America's destiny too, now that it had a cruel and authoritarian man reign as president. She believed that the world needed the wisdom of women rulers, so it could rest and heal from the cycles of invasions, war mongering, and aggression it had experienced for thousands of years. She wished that men would take their tribal laws and bullshit, and shove it where the sun doesn't shine.

After scanning the area around, she raised her phone, looked at the camera, and spilled her heart out.

I got looks, I got brains, and I got talent
I know how to differentiate a wrong
from a motherfucking right.
But... the truth is, it's not easy
to remove the hijab.
Once you start, you've placed
yourself on a pillar.
Once you remove it, people will
accuse you of no longer
following your faith.

Chapter 12

Niran mopped the floor with practiced ease that didn't show that her mind was preoccupied. She did this simple task almost on auto-pilot when, in reality, she was still in shock and tried to figure out how she would cope with Trump's presidency. Four years. Forty-eight months. 208.5 weeks. 1,460 days, and 35,040 hours.

No amount of writing, Googling, Facebooking, cooking, cleaning, or even walking could get her mind off of the idea that America would now have to accept the unacceptable, would have to survive the worst kind of stupidity, moral decay, and madness. There had already been a lot of it during the elections that had led to this man's presidency in the first place.

How did it happen? How could a pathological liar who bragged about committing sexual assault, perpetrated fraud against the students at his so-called university and stiffed his contractors in his failed business endeavors, not to mention disliked blacks and Muslims and other minorities, get to be voted as the ruler of the most powerful country in the world?

It just didn't make sense to her. What did they think he was going to offer, other than a whole lot of political drama, occasional funny Tweets, four more years of watching funny Saturday Night Live skits, and the occasional hilarious moments in his self-admiration talks where he asserted, "Nobody does [fill in the blank] better than I do." From loving the Bible, to having the most toys, respecting women, and building walls. He made outrageous claims about unrealistic projects and international relations.

Niran was so deep in these depressive thoughts that she didn't notice when Hassina approached her with a package. She'd placed some cooked rice in a Tupperware container and several fresh pomegranates in a bag.

"I want you to drop off this food to the neighbors," she told Niran.

Niran looked at her disheveled self. "Now?"

"No, when we're dead and buried," Hassina snapped at her.

Niran dropped the mop and took her mother's wonderful words and carried them with her, along with the package, as she crossed the street to Mary's house. She rang the doorbell, and Teddy barked enthusiastically until Matthew opened the door. Niran watched Teddy race down the hall to the door and stay right at Matthew's feet, wagging his tail at her.

"Don't be afraid," Matthew said, using his foot to block Teddy's path so that he wouldn't go out. "He doesn't bite."

Niran smiled and greeted the adorable dog. She squatted down to pet him, and he snuffled her hand happily. "How can anyone be afraid of such a beautiful animal?" As Teddy rolled over, she scratched his belly with one hand and then looked up at Matthew. "Is Mary here?"

"She's at work," he said.

"Her car is parked in the driveway," Niran said, turning her head toward the car.

"I'm taking her car for a tune-up, so she took my car."

"Oh…well, my mom wants me to give you these." Niran stood up and offered the bag with the food items to him.

Matthew just looked at her and then opened the door wider. He stepped aside and motioned with a slight nod. "You want to come in?"

There was a long silence as they faced each other. The quick, simple, and proper answer to this request should have been "no" but for Niran, this was an opportunity to step out of her small, little world and explore the unknown. She glanced back at her home and saw no one around. She considered the decision, calculated the risks and benefits, and totaled the equation. Teddy was at her feet, cuddling with her and wiggling his tail, inviting her in as well.

She smiled and said, "I guess for a minute."

She entered the house and easily made her way into the kitchen. Matthew and Teddy followed after her. Teddy was beside himself with joy at having a new visitor and let out a lot of barks. Niran and Matthew tried to calm him down by playing with him a bit. In a few minutes, Teddy settled into his "I know you" routine and stopped barking. Eventually, he went into his corner with his favorite chew toy keeping him occupied.

Niran placed the bag on the kitchen counter, and peeked out of the window. She stared hard at her home. It felt strange to view it from this side of the road, as if she was thousands of miles away, looking out from an airplane window at a foreign land.

"It's weird how our homes look so alike," she said.

"Yeah," Matthew said.

Niran noticed the house get quieter and quieter, with only the sounds produced by the refrigerator and lights. She tried not to observe Matthew, to behave as if he didn't exist, but her body wanted to do the exact opposite. Her body automatically flew in the air with all the compounds of nitrogen, oxygen, carbon dioxide, and many other chemicals that she couldn't describe. She felt her heart pounding against her ribcage, like it was destined to burst out. The frolicking hormones would not rest, leading her forward, step by step, closer and closer, in his direction.

"Did you know that Muslims and Christians aren't supposed to get together?" she asked Matthew, who watched her with an amused look. "It's like forbidden—especially for girls."

"Oh, really?" he said, raising an eyebrow.

She was as cool as ice as she walked closer and closer while talking, like she was in a trance. Her feet wouldn't, couldn't stop.

"Like they can date, I suppose, but no way can they get married," she said, knowing that she ought not to partake in such flirtatious conversations. "Of course, if they date, they'll still get in big trouble with their families…"

She stopped and stood in front of him.

"I had no idea," he replied in the same light-hearted manner.

"Yeah, like real, big trouble…"

She was so close now that their bodies touched a little. They didn't move away from each other. The storm inside of her seemed to settle down a bit, as did her breathing, and she let destiny take its course. She closed her eyes, and her body began melting. Matthew slowly pulled her to him and began to kiss her neck. She embraced him, her face sparkling with happiness as she felt his soft and warm lips against her skin. The world, time, everything suddenly seemed to stop, and became quite magical. She forgot all her worries. *If only tomorrow wouldn't come!*

Before his lips touched hers, however, her brain jolted her back into reality. She realized the rules and regulations against a romance between an unwed boy and girl, a Muslim and a Christian. The sergeant who lived across the street, otherwise known to her as Mom, might also sense what was happening and come to pop this dream with a needle, like a child would do to a balloon.

She pushed him away and looked at his face. Disappointed, Matthew dropped his eyes down. They both stood there studying their feet for a while. It was time for her to go home, but she couldn't get herself to leave. Standing this close to Matthew, she experienced real peace.

"Can you still take me for a drive?" Niran asked, breaking the silence.

"Yeah, let's go right now," he said, relieved that she'd switched the subject. He also took it to indicate that she was willing to continue their relationship so that they would be able to kiss one day.

They sat in Mary's car, and she felt somewhat awkward in it. It wasn't the same as his, although it was not too different either. It had a woman's interior though, with its feminine fragrance and a pink, sparkling rosary hanging from the rearview mirror. Niran commented about the more technical differences, and Matthew explained that driving an unfamiliar car would help her gain more skills.

Once they were out on the street, she felt comfortable with the car, and their flirtation began again, with her even initiating it. When Matthew placed his hand on the wheel, she placed hers on top of it and giggled. Matthew only blushed, but he didn't move his hand away, allowing her to be as playful as she wanted to be. His character helped her bold and

145

witty charm to the surface because he embraced it. Around him, her confidence reached its highest peak without any issues, confirming that she was well-versed in the art of flirting even though she wouldn't be considered "experienced."

The phone rang so abruptly that, flustered, Niran tried to answer with fidgeting fingers while still driving, but Matthew stopped her.

"It's illegal to drive and talk on the phone," he warned.

"It's only illegal if there are cops around," she said with a laugh. Matthew grinned, but he still didn't let her answer the phone.

They passed the same billboard she saw when she rode in the back with her parents, the one that featured a beautiful girl with curly, dark hair, smiling at everyone unashamedly.

"Are you going to cover up for World Hijab Day?" Matthew asked.

Niran scowled, confused, and then suddenly burst out laughing as she thought how ridiculous that sounded. An entire day dedicated just for the hijab, which she wore on a nearly 24/7 basis.

"What the hell is that?" she asked.

"I don't know," Matthew said sheepishly. "Some event. I saw it online."

Niran laughed even harder.

"I thought you're into that stuff," he said, embarrassed.

"You've been Googling stuff about my hijab?"

"Well, ah, I…ahhh…" he stammered.

"Cover up?" Niran asked teasingly. "I mean, I'm already covered up, don't you think? Or do you think I don't cover up enough?"

"Yeah, I guess you're covered up."

They both smiled at each other, and an odd happiness engulfed Niran. She felt special. He wanted to learn more about her, which meant his interest went beyond physical attraction.

"You know why women are forbidden to drive in some countries?" she asked.

"Cause they're supposed to have male guardians."

"No. It's because some imams believe that if a woman drives, she'll... you know."

"No, I don't know," he answered.

"Well, can you guess?"

He thought it over for a moment, but he didn't think too hard or too far. "No," he stated.

"She'd, you know, change gears..."

"What?"

Seeing he was genuinely baffled now, Niran searched for the right words, and lastly, she got it. With her hand gripping the gear shift, she said, "Become interested in gear shifts."

Matthew's face reddened as he got the gist of what she had said. They eyed each other intensely, and now, she unexpectedly blushed. She wondered if she'd gone too wild or crazy to pour her emotions into a man's palms as easily as a gardener poured water over a plant. The car was filled with a charged and magnetic energy, and she quietly turned the car back toward her street.

Staring ahead, Niran gasped and then sharply pressed on the brake. The car came to a halt with a jerk. She and Matthew were in stunned horror to see that Hassina was standing in the middle of the street, looking directly at them.

The sandal-flying-in-the-air situation that took place not too long ago reemerged. This time it was in the kitchen and without the presence or assistance of Sermad. Only Ali was there to hold his mother back from walloping Niran with the sandal, and he wasn't able to do much against his mother's rage.

Screaming, Niran dodged her mother's attacks and ran into her room. As quickly as possible, she closed the door and pressed her back against it so that no one could open it. She sat on the ground, pressing her back harder against the door, but she did not weep. She was determined to fight back. *No sandal or rebuke will deter her from her strong will!* She turned to her strength and power, her faith, combined with the act of formulating words into poetry.

> *There's this saying that a woman is weak*
> *When she goes out, Satan seeks to tempt her.*
> *People, get your heads out of the gutter*
> *Give females the respect they deserve.*

Ali remained in the kitchen with his mother, trying to calm her down and understand what was going on. After Hassina stopped flailing about with her sandal in the air, she put her hand on her chest and leaned against the table, gasping for air. As Ali watched, he saw that his mother was nearly passing out. The scene resembled something he had seen before, but he couldn't put his finger on it. Then it clicked.

Not too long ago, he'd watched a sitcom where an old, black man, the main character, clutched his heart whenever

148

he was in trouble, looked to the sky, and cried, dramatically, "Elizabeth, I'm going to join you, honey!" He repeated this performance often enough to where his son realized it was a farce, and therefore, never called the paramedics.

Hassina had a lot of similarities to that old man, true, like wanting sympathy when things weren't going his way. But, Ali couldn't jeopardize his mother's life like that. He couldn't afford to delay much-needed medical attention because he suspected she was *pretending* to have a heart attack like that old man—*oh, what was his name?*

In the end, Ali could not remember the name but he ended up doing the right thing. He called the paramedics. In the blink of an eye, they showed up with their medical supplies. A wave of chaos and commotion ensued, smacking everyone in the face like a freight train.

They carried Hassina out on a stretcher to the ambulance. She was awake, no longer in the passing-out mode, and shouting a lot of Arabic profanities. Ali and Niran stood beside her in sullen silence. Niran observed that, surrounded by the white-dressed paramedics, her mother's body seemed bloated, three-times larger than she actually was. She decided once the drama was over, she'd talk to her about losing weight.

Mary, who had just returned from work, rushed across from the street when she saw them.

"What happened?" she asked, concerned.

Niran saw Matthew watching from afar as she turned to answer Mary, "She got dizzy and passed out."

"Oh my God, I hope it's nothing serious."

"She might've gotten jealous of your mother spending all those days at the hospital," Niran said.

"You seem so calm," Mary said, perplexed.

"You better get back to your work. My mom will be fine. Trust me."

"I came to tell you some good news, but with this situation…"

"What good news?"

"Well, first, the hospital discharged my mother. I'm going to pick her up now. Second, and more important to you, your food stamp application is approved."

Hassina opened her eyes wide and almost seemed to jump out of the stretcher like a ghost, her facial expression full of hope and joy. "Really?" she asked Mary.

Everyone watched in astonishment as she tried to get up. She started unbuckling the straps that were tying her on the stretcher. The paramedics held her down and made all attempts to keep her calm, but there was no use. She behaved as if worms were invading her body, and she began fighting everyone to get free of the stretcher.

"I swear to Allah, if you don't let me up, I'm going to sue you for everything—even the food in your deep freezer," she threatened the paramedics, who were astounded by her behavior.

"Always assuming everyone is afraid of a shortage of food," Niran mumbled, and for the first time in her life, she wondered if she was adopted or switched at birth.

After a lot of back and forth, and once the paramedics were sure that Hassina was not in any danger, the ambulance drove away, and everyone stood in the driveway talking. At this moment, Sermad drove up, his heart beating. He hurried out of his car and approached the family like an Olympic swimmer. Niran and Ali groaned because evidently the family drama was now going to get dragged out for longer. They had been hoping to get inside as soon as possible.

"Why was the ambulance here?" Sermad asked.

"Never mind that," Hassina exclaimed. "Good news! Our food stamps are approved!"

"Oh, seeing that ambulance almost gave me a heart attack," he said. "Well, I have good news too. I got a better job! At a restaurant."

Hassina waved her arms in joyful abandon and howled a piercing ululation. She felt younger than on the day of her wedding as she smelled the aroma of heaven enter her kitchen and the entire house. This was not a simple matter of abundance of food, but a sign that the angels were in close proximity and blessings would continue to come.

Ali suddenly recalled that the old, black man's name on the sitcom was Fred G. Sanford, and his son's name was Lamont.

"Thank God for all this good news," Niran said. "Now, Mom has recovered."

"Recovered?" Sermad asked. "What's wrong?"

No one said a word. The day had been full of ups and downs, and they wanted to avoid further ups and downs. One moment everyone was happy because of Sermad's new job; the next moment, they were sad, remembering that Niran's troubles weren't completely over.

Once dinner was over, and the dishes were washed and put away, the children went to their respective rooms. Hassina sat with Sermad at the kitchen table, drinking tea. Occasionally, she spun the hamsa into the air to ward off any evil spirits. She pondered whether she ought to get a new hamsa since this one was obviously not working properly.

"We need to go back to Iraq," she said to Sermad.

"To the cold days when we drank soup and tea to keep warm in the refugee camps?" Sermad asked. "And the hot days when sand flew into our eyes?"

"What other option do we have? Niran is going to keep shaming us."

Sermad was quiet, deep in thought. Hassina also seemed to be deep in thought.

"I suppose we can send her to Iraq on her own," she said after a little while.

"Are you crazy? There's no future for her there."

"Well, I'm not going to just sit here and let her ruin herself and our reputation," she complained, determined to stand up to him this time. "Yesterday, it was indecent Vazeboog messages, today, it's driving alone with a strange guy. Tomorrow; it'll be something worse."

"Wait, what do you mean driving alone with a strange guy?" Sermad asked.

"I saw her," she said, roasting with indignation. She spun the hamsa faster as if she could erase the evil incident that had already occurred. "She was driving the car, and that boy, Matthew was sitting next to her." She shut her eyes tight, the memory too unbearable to relive. "I made them stop, right in the street. I'm telling you, we have to do something."

While her statement surprised Sermad, he remained silent. Hassina took it to mean that he was in agreement with her and that she was making the right decision.

"But sending her to Iraq is impossible," he said, breaking the silence at the table. "It's criminal."

"It's either that or she gets married," Hassina said with finality.

This alarmed Sermad, who shook his head adamantly. The words she spoke sounded so, so wrong.

"What?" Hassina asked. "Is marriage also an impossible and criminal thing?"

"No, but…"

"No buts, no nothing. Plus, you saw all the choices of suitors I gave her and how she reacted to them."

Sermad didn't know what to say. Going against Hassina was like battling Medusa.

"Marriage will do her a lot of good," Hassina said.

Niran ruminated about what had happened earlier in the day and lay on her bed, writing in her journal. She decided to focus on the positive and only capture what she considered beautiful about her family.

My fondest memories, mid afternoon
in the middle of a hot summer.
Dad has the blinds closed, but the AC on.
Mom makes dad his favorite dish –
Oven baked fish. Dad cuts a
pomegranate into four slices.
We attack it for refreshment after
destroying the fish, lemon and onions.
The day is complete.

She thought many thoughts, about the lovely moments of her childhood, of standing close to Matthew and nearly kissing his soft and warm lips, of the small-mindedness of her mother and father. She wondered where to find a definite place to rest her mind and heart. She wanted to pursue her own light, power, and truth, but it felt like she kept missing her appointment with the actual experience of those elements. She was on the verge of writing another poem when the door opened.

Sermad and Hassina walked in. Her mother looked firm and almost stony. Her father looked like an innocent bird, being dragged to the threshold by a cat.

"It's about time we're honest with you," Hassina said. "How do I say it? You're expired. In English, over the hill. We looked it up."

As Niran waited for her mother to explain herself better, with eyes wide open, she wondered why she wasn't born to a scholar, given how much she loved literature. Someone who would nurture her talents, hopes, and dreams, someone who had a deeper understanding of the arts and a respect for women who followed their own path.

While Niran was contemplating the whys and why nots, Hassina continued with her speech. "So, your father and I decided that you get married. Before the expiration date becomes more expired."

They waited for half-a-minute or so for Niran to respond, but she did not. She was stunned. More than that, she wished to banish them from her ordinary life so that she could blossom into an extraordinary butterfly and fly away to the Garden of Eden. They turned off the light and left the room together. In the dark, Niran turned to the camera on her phone.

In the rebellion land,
they completely and utterly destroyed me.

Pomegranate

Has he spoken it? Does it mean anything?
Has he not spoken in? Does it mean anything?
After he stood there in triumph,
he expelled me from the temples.
He made me fly like a swallow from the window.
My life was consumed.

Chapter 13

The days that followed passed by in a haze for Niran. True to her word, and as proficiently as possible, Hassina got suitors for Niran. Even now, there was one right in front of her. Ahmad, the 28-year-old suitor, came with his relatives to her home. He was one of the more acceptable suitors that had visited. He had a dark mustache and nice physical features. Apart from that, Ahmad had a good-paying job and a family that seemed quite nice and civilized. He may come off as a tad-bit arrogant, but he was too good despite all that, and Niran realized that was the problem.

His family chitchatted over tea, helping themselves to pastries and sunflower seeds. At the same time, they sized up Niran and tried to determine whether she had the stellar physical and central attributes of a wife. Niran sighed. *If beauty is all they're after, they might as well exit the door. I am not the one for them,* she thought.

But what if they weren't simply shallow, visual creatures who failed to explore other important qualities when selecting a partner? In this case, she would honestly be screwed. From the looks of everyone's giddy, excited, and positive expressions, she knew it was the latter. A decision was going to be made today. She was certain that her parents planned to ship her off to this groom's home.

Her family entertained the guests with more refreshments, sweets, and delicacies. The women made the ululation to celebrate. Ahmad's relatives kissed Niran, and Niran played along, pretending that she didn't mind marrying a stranger when she wasn't even sufficiently prepared to share herself with another man, let alone a husband.

She checked out Ahmad with extra care, hoping to fall for him. She stopped at his feet and saw a large hole in his sock. She was happily flabbergasted, thrilled that she'd finally found the deal breaker.

Later that night, after the guests had departed, the family gathered in the living room to discuss the day's events.

"He had a hole in his sock," Niran said immediately when she was asked what she thought of Ahmad.

Ali and Fatima laughed in delight.

Hassina, outraged, glared at the two laughing children to subdue them and then turned her attention to Niran. "Well, we're not going to cross him off because of a hole in his sock. When you marry, I'll teach you to stitch and repair socks. And anyway, we already set the wedding date."

Niran lost her composure at that. "With me getting a driver's license, you ask, 'What's the hurry?' But with marriage, you're like a grenade exploding!"

"This is a great opportunity," Hassina said, ignoring Niran's outburst. "Once you get married, you can get your license, go to college, and have complete freedom."

Niran didn't buy any of that nonsense. Marriage for her meant severely limiting her life. If her husband was strict and religious, she'd need his permission to leave the house. He might even want her to go without contraception, in which case she'd have a million children and spend the rest of her youth pregnant and raising kids. This would stop her from advancing her career and participating in life as she wanted. If he did not have the laid-back attitude of her dad, she would be required to obey his orders and commands, unless they were forbidden by God, such as drinking alcohol or eating pork.

Or, she could learn to acquire the tactlessness and aggressiveness of her mother. Suddenly, it dawned upon her that she was her mother, a younger and modern version of her. The thought horrified her. She decided to go get the mail, just so she could leave the house for a moment or two, to dust off the disturbing thoughts. To lift her mood, she started reciting a few words of poetry. She felt sad, but she was still persevering.

Rising on fearsome wings
You rush to destroy my heart
Raging like thunderstorms
Howling like hurricanes
Screaming like tempests
Thundering, raging, ranting
Droning, whiplashing whirlwinds!
That's what it has felt like since
the day I inhabited your womb!

Niran collected the mail and stopped to look at it. She glanced through the bills, and then something caught her eye. There was a catalog and an enrollment application from Oakland University. Her expression changed, and she happily entered her home and continued to rap words of poetry as she deposited the stack of family mail on the kitchen island and took the college catalog and enrollment application with her. Energized, she said to herself, as she entered her room.

> *I will not be eaten by your ferocious fire*
> *or whipped by your furious commands.*
> *You try to triumph over your children's*
> *human rights and prayers.*

She put the catalog and enrollment application on her night table, flipped through a woman's magazine and then pushed it aside. She was suddenly feeling restless, but it also felt like she had found the answer to her problems.

> *Allah can't even explain your outbursts*
> *Why you carry on so*
> *Imposing upon our fates*
> *When He or She is the only Almighty who dictates?*

She was interrupted by Hassina, who walked in, jiggling her hips and shoulders in a way that almost made Niran burst into laughter. Then to her surprise, Hassina imitated Niran in a poetic voice and started partly rapping.

> *Tomorrow morning Ahmad's mother and sisters too*
> *will come and pick us up so we can start*
> *the wedding preparations.*
> *Be ready! It'll be so much fun for me and you.*

Niran's mirth and laughter died on her lips. She wanted to pull the rug from under her mother's feet, but Hassina stepped out, carrying a sense of empowerment that no one could touch. The repetitive years spent in the kitchen, cooking, kneading, baking, churning, and stirring, had impressed a sign of pride and satisfaction in her accomplishments. Was her mother a different type of Enheduanna, the type that reigned in the kitchen? Though she didn't want to, at that moment, she admired her.

Once her mother left, Niran forgot Enheduanna and the feelings she had for her mother. She remembered the message her mother delivered to her, so she went to the closet and flipped miserably through the hangers, searching for something. As her vision blurred, she quit her search, fell on her knees and wept.

Ali heard Niran sob, and his heart broke. He went up to Hassina and told her, but she simply shooed him away. No one disturbed Niran in her room.

The next day, Hassina waited for Niran to wake up. When she didn't join them for breakfast, she sighed, but didn't say anything. Marriage can be daunting for girls, she knew. She just hoped that by giving her daughter some space, she would feel better and become more accepting of this decision.

By the afternoon, Hassina became impatient and returned to the room. She opened the door and said, "Niran, you have to wake up now, or we'll be late. Ahmad's family is coming, and…"

Hassina stopped dead in her tracks. She saw the bed was empty. On the nightstand, there was only the university catalog and application. Niran's phone and purse were gone. She thought, *My worst nightmare has come true!*

"Niran! Niran!" Hassina yelled, before she ran out of the room. "Sermad, Sermad, Niran is gone!"

With Niran gone, Ali became the family's designated telephone caller. He called Niran's phone numerous times, but each time, the call dropped. Her phone was powered off, or she had blocked this number. In a panic, he dialed 911 and spoke to a police officer who explained that a missing 20-year-old wasn't a priority. Niran was not a minor, and therefore, they couldn't go looking for his sister. After finding out that it had been less than 24 hours since she went missing, the officer became even more dismissive. "Maybe she's just at a friend's place. Did you try calling them first?"

Ali hung up, astounded and furious at their ridiculous policy. But, then, he decided to try their advice. The problem was, Ali didn't know if Niran had any friends. She could only be with Mary, but he didn't have Mary's number. He called Matthew instead, who did not answer his phone. He called him several times, and still, there was no answer. Disheartened, Ali hung up and sent him a message instead. He didn't know what else to do now.

Hassina decided they would find Niran on their own, and she and Sermad hurried to Mary's house.

"What's the matter?" Mary asked, seeing their worried expressions as she opened the door. "What happened?"

"Niran is missing," Hassina cried, trembling in fear. "I went into her room, and she was gone. She didn't say anything to us. Do you know where she could be?"

"No, I haven't seen her for a few days now. I've been really busy with work. Maybe she went for a walk."

"No, we had somewhere to go today, and plus, she took her purse."

Mary tried to think of where Niran could have gone, but she honestly had no clue, so she could not offer them any useful information. They decided to go back home.

"Can you please tell us if you hear anything?" Sermad asked.

"Of course. I'm so, so sorry…" Mary said, and closed the door.

Sermad and Hassina made the short walk back to their home, discouraged.

"What should I do with Ahmad's mother?" Hassina asked.

"Tell her that you can't meet today," Sermad said. "That Niran is sick… of us."

Once they were gone, Mary ran into the kitchen where her mother sat at the table drinking coffee.

"Niran is missing!"

"Missing?" Nisreen asked, surprised.

"Her mother said she wasn't in her room. Her purse and phone are gone too. Her parents just came here asking for information about her."

Nisreen stood up, abandoning the coffee mug on the table. She pressed her palm against the cross on her necklace, and said, "Let's help them search for her. I know you're busy with work, so I'll take Matthew with me." She called out, "Matthew! Matthew!" as she kissed a picture of the Virgin Mary on the wall and made the sign of the cross. Then she started to put on her shoes.

She heard no answer and while looking for the car keys, she turned to Mary. "Go get your brother. We need his help."

Mary sprinted out of the kitchen to go to Matthew's room, and Nisreen stopped for a moment to rub her forehead in agony from the sudden headache. Mary returned to her, breathless. "He's not in his room."

"What?"

"He's not there, and his bed is made."

Nisreen felt awful and fidgeted in distress. *What was happening to the world? Terrorist attacks, shootings, violence in every corner, and now this—my son possibly running off with the neighbor's girl!* She shook off the thought of what might be inevitable and held her breath for the remainder of the day.

In the evening, Niran's family gathered around an unusually quiet kitchen table. There was still no news of Niran. Hassina spun the palm amulet, fast enough that it hit Sermad's eye. He covered his face in pain and cursed beneath his breath while she cried into her hijab. She asked Allah to have mercy on her and her children. True, she complained a lot about them, criticizing the hell out of everything they did and demanding they follow her rules, but she loved them dearly. She would willingly lay down on the highway and let cars drive over her for the sake of their well-being.

She mumbled a lot of incomprehensible words to Allah when the front door opened. The family jumped up in surprise as Niran and Matthew walked in. It was like a small but happy explosion went off, something that resembled the televised fireworks on New Year's Eve. Ali let out a whoop of joy,

Sermad hugged Niran, and Hassina, deliriously happy, felt her body shake in relief. She apologized to Allah for all her past harsh ways and asked for forgiveness. The next minute, however, she came to her senses and became angry.

"Where have you been?" Hassina interrogated, smacking Ali on the head to make him stop being so loud. "We nearly died from worry here."

She then saw Matthew and her anger turned into fury. "Why is he with you? Where were you two?"

Hassina didn't give Niran a chance to respond as she removed her sandal and started to attack her with it. Sermad and Ali tried to stop her and break her away. Then and there, Ali decided that before the next opportunity presented itself, he would throw away all of his mother's sandals, or at the very least, keep them hidden during a conflict. Surprisingly, a part of him admired his mother's "street moves." He was certain that if she had to defend herself on the street, she could tear apart the attacker with the sandal as her only weapon. She could use her sandal to neck whip or palm strike the assailant to disable him. No need for martial arts training.

At that moment, Nisreen and Mary appeared in the kitchen, and the fighting paused. The chaos was replaced with a lot of confusion and awkward silence. No greetings were exchanged as it didn't feel appropriate, given the circumstances. However, Nisreen got straight to the point.

"Matthew, where have you been?" she asked her son, who was standing in a corner.

"These two were together," Hassina said in an accusatory tone.

Nisreen, fuming, removed her sandal and started hitting Matthew with it. Niran couldn't believe her eyes. Barely a minute ago, she had been in his position. Ali and Sermad exchanged uncomfortable looks with each other. They didn't know how to tactfully intervene between Nisreen and her son. Matthew was trying to say something, but he couldn't get a word out or be heard over the noises.

One day Niran would write about it in detail. She would start with something like this: *It was a tall, magnificent, and terrible fight, opening the passes in the mountains, led by the fearless descendants of those who first dug wells on the slopes of the uplands, and crossed the ocean, the wide sea of the sunrise.*

Hassina ordered that someone hand her a butter knife for her disobedient child. Nisreen followed in Hassina's footsteps and requested a butter knife as well. Niran and Matthew exchanged a look of horror. Mary suddenly spoke up and broke the tension as she asked a pertinent question of her brother, "Matthew, how can you be so stupid as to date a Muslim girl?"

"What?" Niran said, her emotions boiling over.

Who there can rival his kingly standing, and say like Gilgamesh, "Am I not the king?" Gilgamesh was his name from the day he was born, two-thirds of him a god and one-third human.

It was exactly the description for the modern Enheduanna, the modern-day Niran, which in the Arabic language translates to "Fire." Yes, she is that fire, the fire which burned all doubts and hesitations, and came for Mary, trying to push past both moms to get to her.

"Someone get me a knife too, a butcher knife!" she yelled, shoving aside her mom, who gripped her tightly. "Mom, get out of my way so I can straighten this girl out."

Niran wanted a weapon; anything would do, but a butter

knife was much too lame. Even a steak knife or a bread knife would be better. It would be interesting to get her hand on that Paleolithic tool created some 2.5 million years ago by humans in Tasmania, and probably first used for hunting, that she'd read about in one book. She would even be happy to use the first, single-edged knife that was made in the Bronze Age 4,000 years ago and used for hunting, cooking, and carpentry.

"I'm so disappointed in you!" Nisreen said, to Matthew, after she was done beating him with her sandal. "So ashamed of you. So…"

"I never touched her," Matthew interrupted, finally able to get a word in, but it seemed to be falling on deaf ears.

Sermad, weary with all the chaos and noise in the kitchen, entered like a lion into the middle of the arena and roared, "Everyone, stop!" His thundering voice made everyone pause.

Slowly, things calmed down, but now, nearly all the women had a butter knife close to their sides.

"You're all jumping to conclusions!" Sermad continued. "Listen to the other side. Give them a chance to explain."

"Allah, give me patience and give it to me now!" Hassina declared.

"Babba, what happened?" Sermad asked Niran gently. "Where were you?"

"I was at McDonald's," Niran said.

"McDonald's?" Hassina asked suspiciously.

Niran nodded her head.

"Oh, habbibti, you were hungry? Is that what this is all about? You should've…" Hassina started lovingly approaching Niran, who instinctively took a step back, afraid of getting in striking distance of her mother's sandals.

"Mom, no! Listen. I went and applied for a job. I got hired on the spot."

Hassina was suspicious again of Niran. "Mamma, listen, you know I'm better than the FBI, even the ZIA, right? Nothing goes past me. I can tell you what happened there, what happened here. I can tell you where you were, and who you were with. Now, who were you really with?" she asked.

Hassina pointed to Matthew as if she was onto something. "Why was he with you?"

"He wasn't."

"When I heard she was missing, I went looking for her," said Matthew. "I called her many times before she picked up. I told her you were worried about her and that she should come home."

Silence settled in the room as the truth sunk in. At last, Hassina said, "Hmmm, well, oh, deep in my heart, I knew nothing happened. I'm better than the FBI, the ZIA. Besides, my daughter is more honorable than the whole world. As for the job, I don't think Ahmad will allow that, and this McDonald's is far from your future home..."

"Mother! I'm not going to marry Ahmad!"

"You don't have a choice!"

"Yes, I do! I want my independence."

"Your who?"

"My independence," Niran repeated, and then turned toward Mary. "But I don't want to be so independent like Ms. Prissy here."

"What's that supposed to mean?" Mary asked.

"It means you stuff your feelings like our moms stuff eggplants, Ms. I-hide-behind-my-work-and-my-prejudices-and-post-romantic-pictures-on-the-wall-and-ignore-my-own-life."

Mary lowered her eyes.

"Meaning what?" Hassina asked.

"Meaning that I don't want to leave my family," Niran said. "I know you wish I was a passive, submissive, good Arab girl, married with four kids and quiet in the kitchen. Sorry, that's not going to happen."

More silence filled the room at Niran's statement. At a loss about what to do, Sermad paced the kitchen. Niran saw this and drew a cup of tea for her father, sat him down at the table and handed him the cup, which he gratefully received. He sipped from it and then rested the cup on his stomach, waiting for the storm to pass and the heat at the base of the cup to settle his upset stomach.

"You can decide to disown me, and you can stop loving me," Niran said. "But that doesn't mean I will stop loving you."

Hassina ignored Niran and turned to Sermad.

"Look at the mess you made," she said.

"Hassina, I feel bad for the kids," Sermad replied. "We bring them here, and then we expect them to live like we're living in the old country."

"Then what do you want? For her to go to college, date guys…" she looked at Matthew with disapproval before continuing. "And live with them before she gets married?"

Sermad sipped his tea. "There's a saying I heard once: Give the ones you love wings to fly, roots to come back and reasons to stay."

"What idiot said that?"

"I think it was the Dalai Lama," Mary said.

"Dolly, who?" Hassina asked.

"A Buddhist," Mary said.

"Yeah, see, we're not Buddhists."

"Hassina, you're not giving your daughter reasons to stay, so please be careful," said Sermad, reprimanding her.

Hassina was uneasy and eyeballed Niran. "I wouldn't mind replacing some of my children."

Sermad put his teacup on the table with such roughness that he startled his family and caught their attention. He sat up straight. "Well, I don't want to lose her or any of my children. We're in this country, and that's it. You must accept it. Otherwise, otherwise…"

"Otherwise, what?" Hassina asked challengingly.

Heads turned to Sermad with suspense, mouths agape. Everyone really wanted to hear what he would do.

"Otherwise, I, too, will find a way to escape from you."

Heads turned to Hassina.

"Are you threatening me?" she asked him.

Heads turned back to Sermad. Everyone was spectating as if it were a tennis match at mid-court. He stood up and straightened his spine.

"Ah, yes… yes, I am," he said.

"Oh, and where will you go?"

For the first time in his married life, Sermad sucked in his gut, tucked in his T-shirt and pulled up his pants. The waistband nearly touched his chest as he took the pants of the family back from Hassina.

"To… to.. to jail," he said. "Yes, to jail. I'll go to jail, if I have to!"

Hassina gasped.

"That's right," he continued. "I'll get free room and board, free meals, TV all day long, and no headache."

There was another silence, a longer one than the times

before. Eyes were on Hassina now. With her arched brow, she looked over Sermad's sucked in gut and pulled up pants. She was turned on. She touched her wedding ring, then her bracelets, as she entered another space.

"Hmm, lucky me, I'm married to you," she said, femininely, almost flirting. "Enough of this nonsense. We better start breakfast, or we'll starve."

"I can't wait for the next Ramadan, so we really do starve sometimes," said Ali.

"Thanks to Allah, now that both your dad and sister work in a restaurant, we'll never have to worry about starving," said Hassina.

"Allah is great!" Sermad said, letting down his gut.

Hassina glanced at his waist and acted like she was going to throw the sandal at him. He winked at her, so seductively that she melted by the show of this sudden masculine affection.

"Why don't you stay for breakfast as well?" Hassina asked Nisreen. "It's been a long day." She turned to her children. "Set up the blanket on the floor."

Niran and Mary went into the garage and fried some Iraqi-style eggs. Niran taught Mary how to pour date syrup over them.

"I hope I didn't hurt your feelings by what I said in there," she said to Mary.

"No, you didn't," Mary said, awkwardly.

"You're a beautiful and smart girl, but you get caught up in helping others and wanting to take a stand for this and that. What about your life?"

Mary lowered her eyes, and for a moment reflected on what she had been avoiding for years—her life.

"What about love?"

"Are you in love?" Mary asked.

"No, I'm in the garage," Niran said.

The girls laughed.

"What changed your mind about McDonald's?" Mary asked.

"Well," Niran began with some hesitation before she quickly decided to be honest and vulnerable. "Once I squashed my pride, I realized McDonald's is a great place to improve my English, meet friends, and serve people."

Mary smiled.

In the living room, Ali, Matthew, and Sermad spread a blanket on the living room floor. In the kitchen, Nisreen talked with Hassina as they worked at the island. Nisreen prepared pomegranates, and later Niran and Mary returned with the fried eggs.

"In Iraq, the pomegranate is a popular fruit with a rich taste and ancient history, even older than the Bible," said Nisreen, almost to herself. "*Rumman*, the Iraqi word for it, is a Hebrew word which means to 'Rise up.' Rabbis have said that since pomegranate does not have flesh, only seeds, that speaks of the blessings of the commandments of God." Nisreen held a pomegranate sliced in half. "A pomegranate is round like the Earth. When you cut it, you see all these membranes. Reminds me of lines and borders on a map."

Niran and Mary stopped to listen. Intrigued, Ali appeared and peeked over his sister's shoulder to join the conversation.

"When the pomegranate seeds spill out, they unveil and uncover the beautiful sameness inside," said Nisreen.

The girls were mesmerized.

Nisreen took this opportunity to continue to teach them about the meaning of a pomegranate. She explained that the main places in the scriptures that mention pomegranates are in association with decorations on the hems of the high priest's robes and the pillars of the temple Solomon built. They are also a part of the Abrahamic Covenant, that of the blessing of prosperity, with each aril having the potential to become a pomegranate tree that bears many fruits. The large number of arils evoke the idea of the massive numbers of God's children, all of whom are precious.

Niran, Mary and Ali listened attentively and with genuine interest.

"So, we are all God's children here on Earth," Niran affirmed with a sense of joy and purpose. "It is up to us to sow good or bad seeds. Do you understand?"

They all took it in silently. Niran nodded as she turned to Ali. "Well, all but the atheist here."

"You never know," Mary said, smiling at Ali. "Atheists could have a change of heart."

Ali was dumbstruck that Mary had dared to flirt with him! He blushed, turning as red as the pomegranate.

"Niran, where's your little sister?" Hassina asked.

"She was just here," Niran said, taken aback and then called for her. "Fatima! Fatima!"

Fatima walked in with Teddy following her. Hassina screamed and ran into one of the other rooms. The rest of the family surrounded Teddy and petted him.

"I felt so bad for him—all alone," Fatima said. "He's been sitting at the window crying for the longest time."

"That's okay, Babba," said Sermad. "You did the right thing."

"What about Mamma?" Fatima asked.

"Put him on a leash in the backyard, and I'll go get her."

Sermad escorted Hassina out of her room, her face red and sweating. She gradually came into the living room. Everyone assured her that Teddy was on a leash outside. Niran picked up the kitchen towel, wiped away her mother's sweat, and kissed her forehead.

"It'll be fine, Mom," Niran said. "We'll be fine."

"Does McDonald's send free food home with you?" Hassina asked, taking the towel from Niran's hand and wiping her neck.

"Not sure," Niran said. "I'll ask them tomorrow."

Hassina burst into tears of joy, and praised God, "Alhumad Allah."

Next to the rest of the breakfast items, the sliced pomegranates were placed neatly on a platter and then on a blanket over the floor. Hassina's family, along with Nisreen, her son and daughter, sat around the food and began to eat. It was a messy meal, but one that was filled with laughter, conversation, and goodwill.

They removed the hard peels of the pomegranate and,

as they bit into the fruit, the seeds fell onto the tray and piled on their laps and blankets. Glistening in the light, they looked just like precious, ruby red jewels. Niran enjoyed eating the pomegranate even more, as the symbolism that Nisreen had shared with them earlier began to strike her. She looked at the fruit more deeply and visualized the womb, and she contemplated the meaning of fertility and eternal life.

Before everyone parted to their respective homes, Hassina and Sermad stood in the garage to briefly discuss their new and expanded household budget. Mary and Ali went to the backyard to play with the neglected Teddy, a perfect chance for them to figure out if they too could cross that tough religious line. Matthew and Niran kept a bigger distance apart than usual to prove that no funny business occurred earlier today.

The young people had a lot to learn, the main thing being if it was possible to fall in love with someone and, at the same time, each maintain their own identity, religion, and ideology.

The next day, Niran walked with purpose, wearing her headphones. The radio announcer introduced Gethen Christine's new song, *Inside*. Niran listened to the moving lyrics that validated her story, the context of her current existence:

So I must ask myself,
If I were to die tomorrow,
Would I be happy about yesterday?
And if I were to be in God's presence,
What loving things about humanity would I say?

With wings I can see clearly,
But without them I don't know how to be,
So I grow them in my core dearly,
All I ever want is to express me...

Little by little, Niran unwrapped the hijab, but she didn't take it off. Her expression became stoic and she stood taller with her shoulders back. She held up her iPhone for a Facebook Live post, and for the first time ever she pressed the Start Live Video button. She confidently uttered her own words of poetry, which she had been rehearsing for what seemed like eternity.

She walked along a distant and rugged road,
full of stairways, and a bygone era.
She was weary, found momentary peace,
and set all her toils on a tablet of stone.
She built the creative energy of holy Inanna,
the Ishtar goddess, and drew nearer to Her,
to channel Her powers,
which no later king could ever copy or abolish!
Goddess of all divine powers,
Righteous Lady of all resplendent light,
Your house illuminated by beams of spiritual love.
Dressed in shimmering stone jewels and stars.

You arise, return to life,
stimulating a new feminine power.

She untied her hijab and, holding it with her fingertips, let it flow behind her like her long hair, now exposed. She tied it around her waist. A big weight that, for too long, had possessed her emotions, pouring down through her hands, legs, and feet and into the earth, was released. It flew away like a falcon.

She gave thanks to her lightness, gifted to her by that part of the universe that was unknowable and full of strength and magic. She had the biggest megaphone, and now she knew how to use it, no longer afraid of what people will think. She felt courageous, and proud of herself. Not too many people could, like her, fight the emotional and mental fight, and do so without hurting a single soul. She looked at the camera and spoke her words with all the divine powers of a goddess.

The person who helped put this story together
is Enheduanna.
My king something never created before.
Did she not give birth to it?
Yes, she did, and I too can dare to have noble ambitions, to create a
brighter future,
to dream and to achieve my dream.
No man or women can stop me. No, not here!

She paused and gave her audience a coy smile before she articulated her last poetic verse for the day.

Hey everyone,
Before I go,
I want to say that, by the way,
I created this Facebook Page
just to fuck with you.

She winked to her audience. Then she lifted her face and took notice of the luminous colors of the sun, and the shadow of the clouds in the sky. She breathed in the sacred air, breathed in her new vision. She felt alive, like a flower blossoming, having now developed and relaxed into the true passion of her existence. She was determined to reject all immoral, male-ego religions and lies, determined to flourish in her life with a clear conscience and the wind in her hair.

Made in the USA
Middletown, DE
23 March 2021